宋詩明理接千載

古今抒情詩三百首
漢英對照

Parallel Reading of 300 Ancient and Modern Chinese Lyrical Poems
(Chinese-English)

■ 著者：林明理　Author：Dr. Lin Ming-Li
■ 譯者：張智中　Translator：Prof. Zhang Zhizhong

天空數位圖書出版

著者簡介
About the Author & Poet

學者詩人林明理博士〈1961-〉,臺灣雲林縣人,法學碩士、榮譽文學博士。她曾任教於大學,是位詩人評論家,擅長繪畫及攝影,著有詩集、散文、詩歌評論等文學專著33本書,包括在義大利合著的譯詩集4本。其詩作被翻譯成法語、西班牙語、義大利語、俄語及英文等多種,作品發表於報刊及學術期刊等已達兩千篇。中國學刊物包括《南京師範大學文學院學報》等多篇。

Dr. Lin Mingli (1961-), poet and scholar, born in Yunlin County, Taiwan, Master of Law, honorary Ph. D. in literature. She once taught at a university and is a poetry critic, and she is good at painting and photography. She is the author of 33 literary books, including poetry collections, prose, and poetry reviews, as well as a collection of translated poems co-authored and published in Italy. Her poems have been translated into French, Spanish, Italian, Russian and English, etc., and over 2,000 poems and articles have been published in newspapers and academic journals.

* 林明理專書 monograph、義大利出版的中英譯詩合著
Chinese-English Poetry Co-author published in Italy
Lin Ming-Li's monographs and co-authored Chinese-English
Poetry collections published in Italy

1. 《秋收的黃昏》*Dusk of Autumn Harvest*
2. 《夜櫻－林明理詩畫集》*Night Cherry - Lin Ming-Li's Poetry Collection*
3. 《新詩的意象與內涵－當代詩家作品賞析》*The Image and Connotation of New poetry — Appreciation of Contemporary Poets*
4. 《藝術與自然的融合－當代詩文評論集》*The Fusion of Art and Nature — Contemporary Poetry Review*
5. 《山楂樹》*Hawthorn Tree*
6. 《回憶的沙漏》*The Hourglass of Memory*
7. 《湧動著一泓清泉－現代詩文評論》*A Fresh Spring Flowing — Modern Poetry Review*
8. 《清雨塘》*Qing Yu Tang*
9. 《用詩藝開拓美－林明理讀詩》*Using Poetry Art to Develop Beauty — Lin Ming-Li's Poetry Reading*
10. 《海頌－林明理詩文集》*Hymn to the Sea — Collection of Lin Ming-Li's Poems*
11. 《林明理報刊評論 1990-2000》*Lin Ming-Li's Newspaper Review 1990-2000*
12. 《行走中的歌者－林明理談詩》*Walking Singer — Lin Ming-Li's Poems*
13. 《山居歲月》*Living in the Mountain*
14. 《夏之吟》*Summer Yin*
15. 《默喚》*Inspiration*
16. 《林明理散文集》*Lin Ming-Li's Essays*
17. 《名家現代詩賞析》*Famous Modern Poetry Appreciation*
18. 《我的歌》*My Song*
19. 《諦聽》*Listening*

著者簡介

20. 《現代詩賞析》 Modern Poetry Appreciation
21. 《原野之聲》 The Sound of the Field
22. 《思念在彼方　散文暨新詩》 Missing in the Other Side of the Prose and New Poetry
23. 《甜蜜的記憶（散文暨新詩）》 Sweet Memory (Prose and new poetry)
24. 《詩河（詩評、散文暨新詩）》，文史哲出版社。 Poetry River (Poetry Criticism, prose and new poetry), History & Philosophy Publishing House.
25. 《庫爾特·F·斯瓦泰克，林明理，喬凡尼·坎皮西詩選》（中英對照） Selected Poems by Kurt F. Swatek, Lin Ming-Li and Giovanni Campisi (Chinese-English)
26. 《紀念達夫尼斯和克洛伊》（中英對照）詩選，義大利：Edizioni Universum（埃迪采恩尼大學），宇宙出版社。 Selected Poems in Memory of Davonis and Chloe (Chinese-English), Italy: Edizioni Universum (University of Ediceni), Cosmos Press.
27. 《詩林明理古今抒情詩 160 首》 Parallel Reading of 160 Ancient and Modern Chinese Lyrical Poems (Chinese-English)
28. 《愛的讚歌》（詩評、散文暨新詩） Hymn of Love (Poetry commentary, prose and New poems)
29. 《埃內斯托·卡漢，薩拉·錢皮，林明理和平詩選》（義英對照） Selected Poems of Ernesto Kahan, Sara Ciampi, Lin Mingli and Heping (Yi-Ying contrast)
30. 《祈禱與工作》（中英義詩集 Prayer and Work
31. 《名家抒情詩評賞》（漢英對照） Appreciation of Lyrical Poems by Famous Poets (Chinese-English)
32. 《山的沉默》 Silence of the Mountains
33. 《宋詩明理接千載——古今抒情詩三百首》，天空數位圖書出版，臺中市。 Parallel Reading of 300 Ancient and Modern Chinese Lyrical Poems (Chinese-English), Sky Digital Books, Taichung City.

譯者簡介
About the Author & Translator

　　張智中，天津市南開大學外國語學院教授、博士研究生導師、翻譯系主任，中國翻譯協會理事，中國英漢語比較研究會典籍英譯專業委員會副會長，天津師範大學跨文化與世界文學研究院兼職教授，世界漢學·文學中國研究會理事兼英文秘書長，天津市比較文學學會理事，第五屆天津市人民政府學位委員會評議組成員、專業學位教育指導委員會委員，國家社科基金專案通訊評審專家和結項鑒定專家，天津外國語大學中央文獻翻譯研究基地兼職研究員，《國際詩歌翻譯》季刊客座總編，《世界漢學》英文主編，《中國當代詩歌導讀》編委會成員，中國當代詩歌獎評委等。已出版編、譯、著 120 餘部，發表學術論文 130 餘篇，曾獲翻譯與科研多種獎項。漢詩英譯多走向國外，獲國際著名詩人和翻譯家的廣泛好評。譯詩觀：但為傳神，不拘其形，散文筆法，詩意內容；將漢詩英譯提高到英詩的高度。

譯者簡介

Zhang Zhizhong is professor, doctoral supervisor and dean of the Translation Department of the School of Foreign Studies, Nankai University which is located in Tianjin; meanwhile, he is director of Translators' Association of China, vice chairman of the Committee for English Translation of Chinese Classics of the Association for Comparative Studies of English and Chinese, part-time professor of Cross-Culture & World Literature Academy of Tianjin Normal University, director and English secretary-general of World Sinology·Literary China Seminar, director of Tianjin Comparative Literature Society, member of Tianjin Municipal Government Academic Degree Committee, member of Tianjin Municipal Government Professional Degree Education Guiding Committee, expert for the approval and evaluation of projects funded by the National Social Science Foundation of China, part-time researcher at the Central Literature Translation Research Base of Tianjin Foreign Studies University, guest editor of *Rendition of International Poetry*, English editor-in-chief of *World Sinology*, member of the editing board of *Guided Reading Series in Contemporary Chinese Poetry*, and member of the Board for Contemporary Chinese Poetry Prizes. He has published more than 120 books and 130 academic papers, and he has won a host of prizes in translation and academic research. His English translation of Chinese poetry is widely acclaimed throughout the world, and is favorably reviewed by international poets and translators. His view on poetry translation: spirit over form, prose enjambment to rewrite Chinese poetry into sterling English poetry.

摘要
Synopsis

　　為了打開讀者進入古詩及新詩的門徑，本書由現任南開大學外國語學院博士生導師張智中教授悉心精選中國宋詩絕句150首，並由臺灣學者林明理博士以新詩150首延伸的方式，嘗試讓海內外熱愛詩歌的讀者，能欣賞到中英對照的詩美意境。我們期盼本書能夠讓閱讀詩歌成為通向每一個讀者心靈愉悅的道路。

著者：張智中、林明理　謹識
2024年9月9日

　　In order for the readers to be acquainted with ancient and modern Chinese poems, this book includes 150 quatrains by Song dynasty (960-1279) poets, which are respectively paired up with modern Chinese poems bLingy Dr. Lin Ming-Li. Thus, the poems total up to 300, which are translated into English by professor Zhang Zhizhong, hopefully to make delightful reading for both Chinese and English readers.

Authors: Zhang Zhizhong; Lin Ming-Li
September 9, 2024

推薦序
Preface

　　美是主觀的感受，不是客觀的評斷。它會因個人的閱歷、教育、環境等因素，而產生不同的體悟，對美不同的看法。也會隨著光陰的流轉，產生不同的變化，誠如赫拉克利圖斯（Herakleitos, 544 - 484 B.C.）所說：「濯足流水，水非前水。」它是吾人的嚮往，一生的追求；也是爭議的起點，和諧的終點。美涵蓋天地萬物，無所不在，萬物本體，藉其形式，展演姿態，讓人欣賞。故美只有美，沒有醜的成分，只有不懂得欣賞的人。美需要知音，才能淋漓盡致的詮釋，否則它也只是個美。

　　美雖有很多種，唯文學之美最讓人揪心，各式各樣的感受都有，它能讓讀者融入其中，隨之起舞，時而血脈賁張、時而黯然銷魂，說到辛酸處，一把鼻涕，一把淚，看到絕妙時，仰天大笑，拍案叫絕，喜怒哀樂盡在表情中。何以如此？因人生有太多的遺憾，世間有太多的不平，文人便藉文學作品的抒發，以獲得心靈的慰藉。它們都是來自作者一次次的自我追尋，是靈魂的吶喊，也是人生的省思，它讓讀者轉化為個人的內省，在千迴百轉的人生旅程中，尋得一片心靈的寧靜與自在。

　　林明理老師就是這樣有魅力的作者，她雖非文學正統科班出身，卻憑著對文學的熱愛，而成為知名的詩人、評論家，在繪畫上也有出色的表現，誠屬難得！林詩人是一個典型的作家，為人正直，不喜奉承，投緣的人，彼此很容易成為知心好友，話不投機，則不屑與之交往，在我們中國文藝協會的人緣，形成兩個極端，就是這種獨特的性格，造就她作品的高度。所以她的作品，樸實不矯作，真誠中還帶點對世間的憐憫，讓人讀來心有戚焉！當然，作品有好、有壞！然一個詩人終其一生，能有幾一名句流傳於世，便能千古風流，更何況，林詩人有不少佳句。魯迅說：「一個人得了讚和，是促其前進，得了反對，是促其奮鬥。」因此，不管本人的評論是好是壞，皆意在勉勵。

至於大陸南開大學翻譯系主任張智中教授，我們同為「世界漢學研究會」的成員，他是本會的理事兼英文秘書長，也是《世界漢學》期刊的英文主編。研究外國語翻譯者不計其數，然能翻譯古典詩詞者，又能翻譯得如此貼近原作者本意，實屬少見。因古典文學向來微言大義，短短幾句卻隱含人生的大道理，如果沒有深厚古典文學的底子，恐難於勝任，可見張主任具備了這兩種能力。

本書之問世，是詩人林明理，學者張智中兩人的絕配，一個善於寫詩，一個善於翻譯，並以《宋詩明理接千載……》為書名，作者善於將自己的名字，來做橋接，串聯成"古今中外之作"，意境之大，不可言喻，在文藝界有此創意者，絕無僅有。還有，封面繪畫設計，皆是作者親為，足見詩人的多才多藝。今有幸，在本書出版前，即能先睹為快，並受其邀約為該書作序，而該書確有收藏價值，值得你我細細品味，故本人樂於推薦。

曹丕說：「蓋文章經國之大業，不朽之盛事。年壽有時而盡，榮樂止乎其身，二者必至之常期，不若文章之無窮。」人生百年，飛逝而過，不管像是王永慶的財富，或是林志玲的美麗，一生榮辱，最後僅剩一堆黃土。生命的短暫，總讓我們有著無限感慨，唯有我們的作品才能千秋萬載的流傳下去，讓後世所景仰，詩人林明理，學者張智中即是成就這麼一個千載流傳的功業。

國立雲林科技大學漢學研究所退休教授
天空出版社社長
蔡輝振　謹識於臺中望日臺
2024.08.28

推薦序

Beauty is a subjective experience, instead of an objective judgment. It varies depending on a person's life experiences, education, environment, and other factors, leading to different perceptions and interpretations of beauty. As time passes by, these perceptions may change, as Heraclitus (544-484 B.C.) said, "No man ever steps in the same river twice, for it is not the same river and he is not the same man." Beauty is something we aspire after as a lifelong pursuit; it is also the starting point of disputes and the endpoint of harmony. Beauty encompasses all things in the world, omnipresent and inherent in everything, manifesting itself in forms which we can appreciate. Thus, beauty is purely beauty, without any element of ugliness, though there are those who fail to appreciate it. Beauty, to be fully understood and expressed, requires a discerning audience; otherwise, it remains merely a form of beauty.

Although there are many kinds of beauty, the beauty of literature is the most prominent and poignant, evoking a wide range of emotions. It can draw readers into its world, making them dance to its rhythm, sometimes causing their blood to race, other times leaving them heartbroken. In sorrowful moments, they may shed tears, and when witnessing something extraordinary, they may laugh out loud, applauding in amazement, with all their emotions displayed on their faces. Why does this happen? Because life is filled with regrets, and the world is full of injustices. Writers express their feelings through literary works to find solace for their souls. These works are born from the author's repeated self-reflection, a cry from the soul, and a contemplation of life. They transform the reader's experience into personal introspection, helping them find a moment of peace and freedom amidst the twists and turns of life's journey.

Dr. Lin Ming-Li is a mesmerizing author. Without a literary background of school education, yet her deep love for literature has made her a renowned poet and critic, and she also excels in painting—a rare accomplishment indeed! Lin, as a poet, is a quintessential writer: upright, she is above flattery. She easily forms close friendship with like-minded individuals, but if she finds no common ground, she has no interest or intention in socializing with them. Her unique personality has created two extremes in her relationships within the Chinese Literary Arts Association, and it is precisely this distinct character that has elevated the quality of her works. Simple and unpretentious, her writing is infused with sincerity and a touch of compassion for the world, which resonates deeply with readers. Naturally, good works are mixed with mediocre ones, but if a poet can create even a few lines which can stand the test of time, he has achieved something extraordinary—and Lin, as a poet, has crafted much more such lines. As Lu Xun once said, "When a person receives praises, it encourages them to progress; when they face criticism, it spurs them to work harder." Therefore, whether my critique is positive or negative, it is meant to encourage and inspire the poet.

As for Professor Zhang Zhizhong, director of the Translation Department at Nankai University in the China mainland, we are both members of the "World Sinology Literary China Seminar". He serves as the director and English secretary-general of the association, as well as the English editor-in-chief of the journal *World Sinology*. There are countless scholars engaged in translation between various languages, but those are rare who can translate classical Chinese poetry into foreign languages in a way that closely aligns with the original poet's intent. Classical literature often conveys profound meanings in a few words, encapsulating deep truth about life. Without a solid foundation in classical literature, it would be difficult to achieve this kind of quality translation. Obviously, professor Zhang possesses both abilities.

推薦序

The fruition of this book is the result of the harmonious collaboration between poet Lin Ming-Li and translator Zhang Zhizhong: one excels at writing poetry, and the other at translation. Jointly, they have produced a work titled *Parallel Reading of 300 Ancient and Modern Chinese Lyrical Poems (Chinese-English)*, where the author is good at using her name as a bridge which connects literary works from ancient to modern times. The artistic conception of this book is vast beyond description, and such creativity is unique in the literary world. Additionally, the cover design and drawings are all by the poet, showcasing her versatile talents. I am lucky to have the opportunity to preview this book before its publication and to be honored to write the preface. This book is of great value, and is worth close reading, so I am pleased to recommend it.

Cao Pi once said, "Literary works are the great undertakings of the nation and events of eternal significance. While life is finite and personal glory & joy end with oneself, literature endures forever." A life of 100 years passes in the blink of an eye: whether it be the wealth of Wang Yung-ching or the beauty of Lin Chi-ling, all the glory and disgrace of life eventually turn to dust. The brevity of life often fills us with boundless reflection, but only our literary works can be passed down through the ages, to be appreciated and admired by the future generations. Dr. Lin Ming-Li and professor Zhang Zhizhong have been working in this direction.

Tsai Huei-Ching
Retired Professor, Institute of Sinology,
National Yunlin University of Science and Technology
President of Sky Digital Books
Wangri Terrace in Taichung
August 28, 2024

宋詩明理搖千載
古今抒情詩三百首
漢英對照

著者暨編譯者導言
Introduction by the Compiler-Translator

　　臺灣學者、詩人林明理博士酷愛詩歌，她從自己所感覺到的與對古詩閱讀的經驗回憶裡進行篩選、組合，欲使其創作的新詩加在編譯的宋詩絕句之後，以期望讀者更貼近地感覺和瞭解詩美的世界。我認為，若能讓古詩和新詩研究同步相輔相成，讓翻譯詩歌的涵義變得更生動活潑，以趨使學生對欣賞詩歌與研讀上產生更大的興趣，這是此書最重要的價值，也可以加深閱讀時的感性和體悟，這也是我們的期許。

張智中
2024 年 9 月 9 日於南開大學外國語學院翻譯系

　　Lin Ming-Li, as a scholar-poet of Taiwan, is a great lover of poetry, and she selects her own poems to be paired up with the quatrains by Chinese poets of Song dynasty, which have similar themes or sentiments, in order for readers to appreciate more thoroughly the beauty of poetry. It is my belief that, if the reading and translation of both ancient Chinese poems and modern Chinese poems can be undertaken simultaneously, the understanding of poetry will be deepened, and poetry translation will be more flexible through enlivening — and the readers' interest in poetry, hopefully, will be greatly heightened.

Zhang Zhizhong
September 9, 2024
Translation Department of the School of Foreign Studies,
Nankai Univeristy

宋詩明理接千載
——古今抒情詩三百首

Parallel Reading of 300 Classical and Modern Chinese Lyrical Poems (Chinese-English)

詩歌是百花之蜜、知識的精華、智慧的本質、天使的言語。

（英國詩人納許）

Poetry is the nectar of flowers, the cream of knowledge, the essence of wisdom, and the words of angels.

— By Graham William Nash, British poet

目錄
Table of Contents

1. 春日（朱熹）A Fine Day in Spring (Zhu Xi)
   春歸（林明理）Returning of Spring (Lin Ming-Li) ·········· 30
2. 觀書有感（朱熹）On Reading (Zhu Xi)
   凝（林明理）Gaze (Lin Ming-Li)·················· 31
3. 題榴花（朱熹）To Pomegranate Flowers (Zhu Xi)
   夏至清晨（林明理）The Morning of Summer Solstice
   (Lin Ming-Li) ·················· 32
4. 元日（王安石）The Spring Festival (Wang Anshi)
   在白色的森林下面（林明理）Under the White Forest
   (Lin Ming-Li) ·················· 34
5. 梅花（王安石）Plum Blossoms (Wang Anshi)
   冬之戀（林明理）The Love of Winter (Lin Ming-Li)········ 36
6. 泊船瓜州（王安石）Anchor My Boat at Guazhou (Wang Anshi)
   在那星星上（林明理）Over the Stars (Lin Ming-Li)········ 37
7. 書湖陰先生壁（王安石）Written on the Wall of My Neighbor
   (Wang Anshi)
   靜寂的黃昏（林明理）Silent Dusk (Lin Ming-Li) ·········· 38
8. 登飛來峰（王安石）The Peak of Flight (Wang Anshi)
   寂靜的遠山（林明理）The Silent Remote Mountain
   (Lin Ming-Li) ·················· 39
9. 遊鐘山（王安石）Touring the Bell Mountain (Wang Anshi)
   致青山（林明理）To the Green Mountain (Lin Ming-Li)········ 41
10. 江上（王安石）On the River (Wang Anshi)
    季雨來了（林明理）The Rainy Season Is Coming (Lin Ming-Li) ··· 42
11. 鐘山即事（王安石）Life in the Bell Mountain (Wang Anshi)
    山的呢喃（林明理）Whisper of the Mountain (Lin Ming-Li) ··· 44

目錄

12. 夜吟（陸遊）Composing Poems in the Depth of Night (Lu You)
    夜之聲（林明理）Sound of the Night (Lin Ming-Li) ········ 45
13. 示兒（陸遊）My Will to My Son (Lu You)
    我哭，在西牆（林明理）I Weep Against the West Wall (Lin Ming-Li) ··· 47
14. 冬夜讀書示子聿（陸遊）To My Son When Reading in a Winter Night (Lu You)
    冬之歌（林明理）Winter Song (Lin Ming-Li) ············· 49
15. 劍門道中遇微雨（陸遊）Caught in a Drizzle on the Way (Lu You)
    十月秋雨（林明理）Autumn Rain of October (Lin Ming-Li) ··· 50
16. 秋懷（陸遊）A Tinge of Emotion at Autumn (Lu You)
    秋的懷念（林明理）The Fond Memory of Autumn (Lin Ming-Li) ··· 52
17. 十一月四日風雨大作（陸遊）Composed in a Rainstorm (Lu You)
    重複的雨天（林明理）Rainy Days Which Repeat Themselves (Lin Ming-Li) ··· 53
18. 沈園二首（其一）（陸遊）Two Poems Composed in Shen Garden: for My Former Wife (1) (Lu You)
    晚秋（林明理）Late Autumn (Lin Ming-Li) ················ 56
19. 沈園二首（其二）（陸遊）Two Poems Composed in Shen Garden: for My Former Wife (2) (Lu You)
    寒夜的奇想（林明理）Cold Night Fantasy (Lin Ming-Li) ···· 58
20. 春思（方嶽）Spring Wind (Fang Yue)
    春雪——致吾友張智中教授（林明理）Spring Snow — To My Friend Professor Zhang Zhizhong (Lin Ming-Li) ······ 60
21. 農謠五首（其一）（方嶽）Ballads (No. 1 of 5 poems) (Fang Yue)
    海波親吻了向晚的霞光（林明理）The Waves Kiss the Evening Glow (Lin Ming-Li) ································· 63
22. 江上（劉子翬）On the Autumn River (Liu Zihui)
    冬日的魔法（林明理）The Magic of Winter (Lin Ming-Li) ··· 65

17

23. 汴京紀事二十首（其五）（劉子翬）Twenty Poems about Reminiscences in the Capital of Bianjing (No. 5 of 20 poems) (Liu Zihui)
九份之夜（林明理）The Night of Jiufen (Lin Ming-Li) ······ 66

24. 遊園不值（葉紹翁）Failing to Meet a Friend (Ye Shaoweng)
在山丘的彼方（林明理）On the Other Side of the Hill (Lin Ming-Li) ·············· 68

25. 夜書所見（葉紹翁）View of an Autumn Night (Ye Shaoweng)
細密的雨聲（林明理）The Dense Rain (Lin Ming-Li) ······ 70

26. 雪梅（盧梅坡）Mume Flowers & Snowy Blossoms (Lu Meipo)
北京湖畔遐思（林明理）Fantasy by the Lake of Beijing (Lin Ming-Li) ·············· 71

27. 夏意（蘇舜欽）The Height of Summer (Su Shunqin)
塞哥維亞舊城（林明理）The Old Town of Segovia (Lin Ming-Li) ·············· 73

28. 淮中晚泊犢頭（蘇舜欽）Mooring in the Evening at Riverside Dutou (Su Shunqin)
遠方的思念（林明理）Yearning From Afar (Lin Ming-Li) ····· 75

29. 和淮上遇便風（蘇舜欽）Sailing on Huaihe River in the Tail Wind (Su Shunqin)
四月的夜風（林明理）The Night Wind of April (Lin Ming-Li) ·············· 77

30. 微涼（寇準）Slight Cool (Kou Zhun)
馬丘比丘之頌（林明理）Ode to Machu Picchu (Lin Ming-Li) ·············· 79

31. 夏日（寇準）The Early Summer (Kou Zhun)
黃昏（林明理）Dusk (Lin Ming-Li) ·············· 80

32. 畫眉鳥（歐陽修）The Blackbird (Ouyang Xiu)
這一夏夜（林明理）This Summer Night (Lin Ming-Li) ····· 81

33. 別滁（歐陽修）Demoted to Chuzhou (Ouyang Xiu)
霧起的時候（林明理）When the Fog Is Rising Up (Lin Ming-Li) ·············· 83

目錄

34. 豐樂亭遊春三首（其三）（歐陽修）Spring Excursion to the Pleasure Pavilion (No. 3 of 3 poems) (Ouyang Xiu)
你的微笑是我的微風（林明理）Your Smile Is a Breeze for Me (Lin Ming-Li) ·················· 84

35. 和梅聖俞杏花（歐陽修）In Reply to Mei Yaochen About Apricot Flowers (Ouyang Xiu)
早櫻（林明理）Early Cherry Blossoms (Lin Ming-Li) ········ 86

36. 夏日絕句（李清照）A Quatrain Composed in Summer (Li Qingzhao)
在白色的夏季裡（林明理）In the White Summer (Lin Ming-Li) ·················· 87

37. 偶成（李清照）A Random Piece (Li Qingzhao)
海上的中秋（林明理）Mid-Autumn at the Sea (Lin Ming-Li) ···· 89

38. 渡漢江（宋之問）Crossing River Han (Song Zhiwen)
炫目的綠色世界（林明理）The Dazzling Green World (Lin Ming-Li) ·················· 91

39. 贈劉景文（蘇軾）To My Friend Liu Jingwen (Su Shi)
岸畔之樹（林明理）The Trees Along the Bank (Lin Ming-Li) ····· 92

40. 六月二十七日望湖樓醉書（蘇軾）Tipsy at Lake-view Pavilion (Su Shi)
愛情似深邃的星空（林明理）Love Is Like the Profound Starry Sky (Lin Ming-Li) ·················· 94

41. 中秋月（蘇軾）The Mid-autumn Moon (Su Shi)
秋的懷念（林明理）The Memory of Autumn (Lin Ming-Li) ····· 96

42. 題西林壁（蘇軾）The True Aspect of Lushan Mountain (Su Shi)
森林之歌（林明理）Song of the Forest(Lin Ming-Li) ········ 97

43. 飲湖上初晴後雨（蘇軾）The West Lake: Sunny or Rainy (Su Shi)
西子灣夕照（林明理）Sunset Over the West Lake Bay (Lin Ming-Li) ·················· 99

44. 春宵（蘇軾）A Spring Night (Su Shi)
默喚（林明理）Silent Calling (Lin Ming-Li) ··············· 100

45. 海棠（蘇軾）Chinese Crabapple Flowers (Su Shi)
在愉悅夏夜的深邃處（林明理）In the Depth of a Pleasant Summer Night (Lin Ming-Li) ……………………… 102

46. 惠崇《春江曉景》（蘇軾）A Spring Scene by the River (Su Shi)
三月的微風（林明理）The Gentle Wind of March (Lin Ming-Li) ……………………………………… 104

47. 花影（蘇軾）Flowery Shadows (Su Shi)
月河把我帶進夢鄉（林明理）The Moon River Brings Me Into My Dreamland (Lin Ming-Li) …………… 106

48. 東欄梨花——和孔密州五絕之一（蘇軾）Pear Blossoms in My Courtyard (Su Shi)
所謂永恆（林明理）The So-called Eternity (Lin Ming-Li) ·· 109

49. 琴詩（蘇軾）On the Chinese Lute (Su Shi)
平靜的湖面（林明理）The Calm Lake (Lin Ming-Li) …… 110

50. 縱筆三首（其一）（蘇軾）Three Random Pieces (1) (Su Shi)
當你變老（林明理）When You Are Old (Lin Ming-Li) ……111

51. 題臨安邸（林升）Written in an Inn of the New Capital (Lin Sheng)
黃昏，賽納河（林明理）Dusk, Seine River (Lin Ming-Li) ·· 113

52. 曉出淨慈寺送林子方（楊萬里）The Charming West Lake (Yang Wanli)
西湖，你的名字在我的聲音裡（林明理）West Lake, Your Name Is in My Voice (Lin Ming-Li) ……………… 115

53. 小池（楊萬里）A Small Pond (Yang Wanli)
靜靜的湖（林明理）The Quiet Lake (Lin Ming-Li) ……… 117

54. 閒居初夏午睡起二絕句（其一）（楊萬里）Waking Up From an Early Summer Nap (No. 1 of 2 poems) (Yang Wanli)
初夏（林明理）The Early Summer (Lin Ming-Li) ………… 118

55. 小雨（楊萬里）A Slight Rain (Yang Wanli)
秋雨，總是靜靜地下著……（林明理）Autumn Rain Always Falls Quietly……(Lin Ming-Li) …………………… 122

目錄

56. 池州翠微亭（岳飛）The Green Pavilion (Yue Fei)
    倒影（林明理）Reflection (Lin Ming-Li) ················ 124
57. 約客（趙師秀）Waiting in Simple Idleness for My Playmate (Zhao Shixiu)
    冥想（林明理）Meditation (Lin Ming-Li) ················ 126
58. 春日偶成（程顥）An Impromptu Poem on a Spring Day (Cheng Hao)
    雲淡，風清了（林明理）The Clouds Are Pale and the Winds Are Crisp (Lin Ming-Li) ················ 128
59. 秋月（程顥）The Autumn Moon (Cheng Hao)
    秋之楓（林明理）The Maples of Autumn (Lin Ming-Li) ··· 130
60. 題淮南寺（程顥）Inscription on Huinan Temple (Cheng Hao)
    樹林入口（林明理）Entrance to the Woods (Lin Ming-Li) ··· 131
61. 江上漁者（范仲淹）A Riverside Fisherman (Fan Zhongyan)
    渡口（林明理）The Ferry (Lin Ming-Li) ················ 133
62. 出守桐廬道中（范仲淹）An Outing (Fan Zhongyan)
    春草（林明理）Spring Grass (Lin Ming-Li) ············· 135
63. 蠶婦（張俞）A Silk-woman (Zhang Yu)
    江岸暮色（林明理）The River Shore Veiled in Dusk (Lin Ming-Li) ················ 137
64. 陶者（梅堯臣）The Potter-worker (Mei Yaochen)
    山間小路（林明理）A Path in the Mountain (Lin Ming-Li) ··· 138
65. 寒菊（鄭思肖）Cold Chrysanthemums (Zheng Sixiao)
    在瀟瀟的雪夜（林明理）A Snowy Night Noisy with Wind (Lin Ming-Li) ················ 140
66. 梅（王淇）The Plum Flower (Wang Qi)
    禪月（林明理）The Moon of Zen (Lin Ming-Li) ············· 142
67. 湖上（徐元傑）On the West Lake (Xu Yuanjie)
    光之湖（林明理）The Lake of Light (Lin Ming-Li) ········ 143
68. 村晚（雷震）A Village at Eventide (Lei Zhen)
    霧（林明理）Fog (Lin Ming-Li) ················ 145

69. 清明（王禹偁）Pure Brightness Day (Wang Yucheng)
    在我的眼睛深處（林明理）In the Depth of My Eyes
    (Lin Ming-Li) ·· 146
70. 初夏游張園（戴敏）Visiting Parks in Early Summer
    (Dai Min)
    夏荷（林明理）Summer Lotus (Lin Ming-Li) ············ 149
71. 七夕（楊樸）Double Seventh Eve (Yang Pu)
    秋夕（林明理）Autumn Eve (Lin Ming-Li) ··············· 150
72. 夜坐（張耒）A Night View (Zhang Lei)
    雨夜（林明理）The Rainy Night (Lin Ming-Li) ·········· 152
73. 牧童詩（黃庭堅）The Herd-boy: a Gainer of Life
    (Huang Tingjian)
    稻草人（林明理）The Scarecrow (Lin Ming-Li) ·········· 154
74. 上蕭家峽（黃庭堅）Going to Xiaojia Gorge (Huang Tingjian)
    正月的融雪（林明理）The Thawing Snow of the Second
    Moon (Lin Ming-Li) ······································ 156
75. 睡起（黃庭堅）Awake from a Sleep (Huang Tingjian)
    貓尾花（林明理）The Cattail Flower (Lin Ming-Li) ······ 157
76. 夜發分寧寄杜澗叟（黃庭堅）Night Journey to Fenning
    (Huang Tingjian)
    想念的季節（林明理）The Season of Yearning
    (Lin Ming-Li) ··· 158
77. 題陽關圖二首（其一）（黃庭堅）Two Poems on the
    Painting of the Sunny Pass (1) (Huang Tingjian)
    夜思（林明理）Night Thoughts (Lin Ming-Li) ··········· 160
78. 到桂林（黃庭堅）In Guilin (Huang Tingjian)
    致摯友（林明理）To my best friend (Lin Ming-Li) ······· 163
79. 雨中登岳陽樓望君山二首（其一）（黃庭堅）Watching
    Junshan Mountain Opposite Yueyang Tower in the Rain (No. 1
    of 2 poems) (Huang Tingjian)
    靜湖（林明理）The Quiet Lake (Lin Ming-Li) ············ 164

80. 雨中登陽樓望君山二首（其二）（黃庭堅）Watching Junshan Mountain Opposite Yueyang Tower in the Rain (No. 2 of 2 poems) (Huang Tingjian)
   寒風吹起（林明理）The Cold Wind Is Blowing (Lin Ming-Li) ·· 166
81. 憶錢塘江（李覯）In Remembrance of Qiantang River (Li Gou)
   四草湖中（林明理）In the Sicao Lake (Lin Ming-Li) ······ 168
82. 鄉思（李覯）Homesickness (Li Gou)
   惦念（林明理）Solicitousness (Lin Ming-Li) ············ 170
83. 城南（曾鞏）The Southern Suburb (Zeng Gong)
   山居歲月（林明理）Years in the Mountain (Lin Ming-Li) ·· 172
84. 宿濟州西門外旅館（晁端友）In a Hotel (Chao Duanyou)
   黃昏雨（林明理）Rain at Dusk (Lin Ming-Li) ············ 173
85. 曉霽（司馬光）A Fine Morning After the Night Rain (Sima Guang)
   拂曉時刻（林明理）At Daybreak (Lin Ming-Li) ············ 175
86. 泗州東城晚望（秦觀）An Evening View at the Suburb (Qin Guan)
   問愛（林明理）About Love (Lin Ming-Li) ·················· 177
87. 春日（秦觀）A Spring Day (Qin Guan)
   冬之雪（林明理）Winter Snow (Lin Ming-Li) ············· 179
88. 秋日（秦觀）An Autumn Day (Qin Guan)
   寂靜蔭綠的雪道中（林明理）Along the Lonely and Green Shaded Snowy Path (Lin Ming-Li) ·················· 180
89. 金山晚眺（秦觀）An Evening View from the Golden Hill (Qin Guan)
   海影（林明理）The Shadow of the Sea (Lin Ming-Li) ······ 182
90. 禾熟（孔平仲）Ripening Crops (Kong Pingzhong)
   憶夢（林明理）Memory of a Dream (Lin Ming-Li) ·········· 184
91. 寄內（孔平仲）To My Wife (Kong Pingzhong)
   無言的讚美（林明理）Wordless Praise (Lin Ming-Li) ······ 186

92. 村居（張舜民）Village Life (Zhang Shunmin)
    夕陽，驀地沉落了（林明理）The Setting Sun Sinks Down Suddenly (Lin Ming-Li) ················ 188
93. 野步（賀濤）A Field Stroll (He Zhu)
    小雨（林明理）Slight Rain (Lin Ming-Li) ················ 190
94. 棲禪暮歸書所見二首（其一）（唐庚）Evening Return into the Zen Mountain (1) (Tang Geng)
    雨影（林明理）The Shadow of Rain (Lin Ming-Li) ········ 192
95. 棲禪暮歸書所見二首（其二）（唐庚）Evening Return into the Zen Mountain (2) (Tang Geng)
    曾經（林明理）Once (Lin Ming-Li) ················ 194
96. 十七日觀潮（陳師道）Watching Tide in Summer (Chen Shidao)
    夜航（林明理）Night Navigation (Lin Ming-Li) ············ 196
97. 春遊湖（徐俯）Spring Excursion to the Lake (Xu Fu)
    春已歸去（林明理）Vanished Spring (Lin Ming-Li) ······· 198
98. 聞笛（劉吉甫）Hearing the Fluting (Liu Jifu)
    春風，流在百草上（林明理）Spring Wind Flowing Over Grasses (Lin Ming-Li) ················ 200
99. 九絕為亞卿作（其一）（韓駒）Nine Quatrains Composed When Touched by the Love Story of My Friend (1) (Han Ju)
    瓶中信（林明理）Bottled Message (Lin Ming-Li) ·········· 202
100. 九絕為亞卿作（其二）（韓駒）Nine Quatrains Composed When Touched by the Love Story of My Friend (2) (Han Ju)
    晚秋（林明理）Late Autumn (Lin Ming-Li) ················ 204
101. 三衢道中（曾幾）Along the Way (Zeng Ji)
    頌黃梅挑花（林明理）In Praise of Yellow Plum Cross-cut (Lin Ming-Li) ················ 206
102. 春日即事（李彌遜）A Dusk in Spring (Li Mixun)
    歌飛阿里山森林（林明理）Songs Fill the Forest of Mt. Ali (Lin Ming-Li) ················ 208
103. 襄邑道中（陳與義）All the Way Down the River (Chen Yuyi)
    永懷星雲大師（林明理）Eternal Memory of Master Hsing Yun (Lin Ming-Li) ················ 210

104. 初夏（朱淑真）The Early Summer (Zhu Shuzhen)
夏日慵懶的午後（林明理）This Lazy Summer Afternoon (Lin Ming-Li)··· 212

105. 除夜自石湖歸苕溪（其二）（姜夔）Going Home from the Stone Lake On New Year's Eve (2) (Jiang Kui)
我願是隻小帆船（林明理）I Wish I Were a Small Sailboat (Lin Ming-Li)··· 214

106. 橫溪堂春曉（虞似良）A Spring Morning (Yu Siliang)
觀白鷺（林明理）An Egret (Lin Ming-Li)··················· 217

107. 早作二首（其一）（裘萬頃）View of an Autumn Morning (1) (Qiu Wanqing)
我要回到從前（林明理）I Want to Be Back to the Past (Lin Ming-Li)··· 218

108. 秋齋即事（許棐）My Study in Autumn (Xu Fei)
穿過無數光年的夢（林明理）The Dream Through Countless Light Years (Lin Ming-Li)··················· 220

109. 夜歸（周密）Night Return (Zhou Mi)
母親的微笑（林明理）Mother's Smile (Lin Ming-Li)···· 222

110. 雷峰夕照（尹廷高）Leifeng Pagoda Caught in the Sunset (Yin Yangao)
愛，是無可比擬的（林明理）Incomparable Is Love (Lin Ming-Li)··· 224

111. 淙淙（王令）Flimsy Clouds (Wang Ling)
AI 的世界將來到（林明理）The World of AI Is Around the Conner (Lin Ming-Li)······························· 226

112. 浪花（王寀）Sprays (Wang Shen)
在一片沙海中（組詩）（林明理）At a Sandy Sea (group poems) (Lin Ming-Li)····························· 230

113. 黯淡院（賈青）The Gloomy Courtyard (Jia Qing)
大磡堡彼岸（林明理）Beyond the Great Barrier Reef (Lin Ming-Li)··· 233

114. 花院（趙與滂）A Flowery Courtyard (Zhao Yupang)
夏日已逝（林明理）Summer Is Gone (Lin Ming-Li)····· 236

115. 題畫（李唐）On Painting (Li Tang)
淵泉（林明理）The Deep Spring (Lin Ming-Li) ·········· 238
116. 春遊吟（吳沆）Spring Outing (Wu Hang)
記夢（林明理）Recalling a Dream (Lin Ming-Li) ········· 239
117. 牽牛花（陳宗遠）The Morning Glory (Chen Zongyuan)
我瞧見……（林明理）I Saw…… (Lin Ming-Li) ········· 241
118. 雨後池上（劉攽）The Pool After the Rain (Liu Ban)
我不歎息、注視和嚮往（林明理）I Don't Sigh, Look and Long For (Lin Ming-Li) ················ 243
119. 題西林壁（蘇軾）The True Aspect of Lushan Mountain (Su Shi)
玉山頌（林明理）Ode to Yushan (Lin Ming-Li) ·········· 245
120. 六月二十七日望湖樓醉書五絕（其一）（蘇軾）Tipsy at Lake-view Pavilion (1) (Su Shi)
北極燕鷗（林明理）The Arctic Tern (Lin Ming-Li) ······· 246
121. 飲湖上初晴後雨（蘇軾）The West Lake: Sunny or Rainy (Su Shi)
金池塘（林明理）The Golden Pond (Lin Ming-Li) ········ 248
122. 海棠（蘇軾）Crabapple Flowers (Su Shi)
金風鈴（林明理）Golden Chimes (Lin Ming-Li) ·········· 250
123. 橫塘（范成大）Hengtang Road (Fan Chengda)
在思念的角落（林明理）In a Corner of Yearning (Lin Ming-Li) ················ 251
124. 寄題西湖並送淨慈顯老（范成大）To the West Lake and the Monk (Fan Chengda)
九份黃昏（林明理）Dusk in Jiufen (Lin Ming-Li) ········ 255
125. 畫眉鳥（歐陽修）The Blackbird (Ouyang Xiu)
棕熊（林明理）The Brown Bear (Lin Ming-Li) ·········· 256
126. 夏日田園雜興十二首（其一）（范成大）Miscellanies of the Four Seasons (1) (Fan Chengda)
與主說話（林明理）Words With My Lord (Lin Ming-Li) 258

目錄

127. 除夜自石湖歸苕溪（其一）（姜夔）Going Home from the Stone Lake On New Year's Eve (1) (Jiang Kui)
長長的思念（林明理）Long-lasting Longing (Lin Ming-Li) ⋯ 260

128. 除夜自石湖歸苕溪（其二）（姜夔）Going Home from the Stone Lake On New Year's Eve (2) (Jiang Kui)
春語（林明理）Words of Spring (Lin Ming-Li) ⋯⋯⋯⋯ 262

129. 夏日（寇準）The Early Summer (Kou Zhun)
遠方的思念（林明理）Longing From Afar (Lin Ming-Li) ⋯ 264

130. 淮中晚泊犢頭（蘇舜欽）Mooring in the Evening at Riverside Dutou (Su Shunqin)
春雨（林明理）Spring Rain (Lin Ming-Li) ⋯⋯⋯⋯⋯ 266

131. 鄉思（李覯）Homesickness (Li Gou)
懷鄉（林明理）Homesickness (Lin Ming-Li) ⋯⋯⋯ 268

132. 碧湘門（陶弼）The Green City Gate (Tao Bi)
白冷圳之戀（林明理）Love of the Bethlehem Ditch (Lin Ming-Li) ⋯⋯⋯⋯⋯⋯⋯⋯⋯⋯⋯⋯⋯⋯⋯ 270

133. 西樓（曾鞏）In the West Tower (Zeng Gong)
短詩十帖（林明理）Ten Short Poems (Lin Ming-Li) ⋯⋯ 272

134. 延州（沈括）The Border Town of Yanzhou (Shen Kuo)
冬之雪（林明理）Winter Snow (Lin Ming-Li) ⋯⋯⋯⋯ 276

135. 曉霽（司馬光）A Fine Morning After the Night Rain (Sima Guang)
拂曉之前（林明理）Before Dawn (Lin Ming-Li) ⋯⋯⋯ 277

136. 夢（呂本中）A Dream (Lü Benzhong)
星夜（林明理）The Starry Night (Lin Ming-Li) ⋯⋯⋯⋯ 279

137. 慶全庵桃花（謝枋得）Peach Flowers at a Small Buddhist Temple (Xie Fangde)
黑夜無法將你的光和美拭去（林明理）The Dark Night Fails to Wipe Out Your Beauty and Light (Lin Ming-Li) ⋯⋯⋯ 281

138. 春晴（王安石）A Fine Spring Day (Wang Anshi)
愛在德爾斐（林明理）A Fine Spring Day (Lin Ming-Li) ⋯ 283

139. 曉行（孔平仲）A Morning Tour（Kong Pingzhong）
科隆大教堂（林明理）Cologne Cathedral (Lin Ming-Li) ⋯ 285

27

140. 樓禪暮歸書所見二首（其二）（唐庚）Evening Return into the Zen Mountain (2) (Tang Geng)
頌長城（林明理）Ode to the Great Wall (Lin Ming-Li) ··· 286

141. 明月溪（滿執中）Moonlit Creek (Man Zhizhong)
塞哥維亞舊城（林明理）The Old Town of Segovia (Lin Ming-Li) ·· 289

142. 書壽昌驛（程俱）An Autumn Scene (Cheng Ju)
黑面琵鷺（林明理）Black-faced Spoonbill (Lin Ming-Li) ·· 290

143. 新泉（黃庭堅）A New Mouth of Spring (Huang Tingjian)
濁水溪星夜（林明理）A Starry Night at Zhuoshui Stream (Lin Ming-Li) ·· 292

144. 春草（劉敞）Spring Grass (Liu Chang)
愛的讚頌（林明理）In Praise of Love (Lin Ming-Li) ····· 294

145. 晚春途中（張公庠）En Ruote in Late Spring (Zhang Gongxiang)
在愛情來臨之前（林明理）Before the Advent of Love (Lin Ming-Li) ·· 295

146. 雙燕（范成大）Twin Swallows (Fan Chengda)
曾經（林明理）Once (Lin Ming-Li) ························ 298

147. 夜雨（呂本中）The Night Rain (Lü Benzhong)
短詩一束（林明理）A Bunch of Short Poems (Lin Ming-Li) ·· 299

148. 江上（俞桂）On the River (Yu Gui)
你一直在我身邊（林明理）You are always by my side (Lin Ming-Li) ·· 302

149. 松雪（嚴粲）Snow on Pine Trees (Yan-chan)
短詩五首（林明理）Five Short Poems (Lin Ming-Li) ···· 304

150. 雪夜（趙葵）A Snowy Night (Zhao Kui)
光點（林明理）Dots of Light (Lin Ming-Li) ··············· 306

附錄：評蔡輝振的《魯迅小說研究》（林明理）
Comments on Tsai, Huei-Cheng's *Studies Of The Novels By Lu Xun* (Lin Ming-Li) ·· 309

宋詩明理接千載

古今抒情詩三百首

漢英對照

宋詩明理接千載
古今抒情詩三百首
漢英對照

1.

春日 　　　　　　　　　　　　　　　朱熹

勝日尋芳泗水濱，無邊光景一時新。
等閒識得東風面，萬紫千紅總是春。

A Fine Day in Spring　　　　　　　Zhu Xi

In a fine day I am in search
　of the beauties of nature
　　by River Sishui; the bound-

less view is stirring, heartening,
　refreshing, uplifting. It is
　　easy to descry the visage

of spring: a riot of colors
　are gorgeous in the east wind
　　which is warm and balmy.

春歸 　　　　　　　　　　　　　　　林明理

轉瞬間
雪變成了馥郁的季節
我在草綠間尋覓
飛掠而過的蝶影
吻走最後一滴星淚

Returning of Spring　　　　　　　Lin Ming-Li

In the blink of an eye
The snow has turned into a season flowing with fragrance

In the green grass I am in search of
The shadows of butterflies flying by
To kiss away the last teardrop from the stars

2 •

觀書有感  朱熹

半畝方塘一鑑開，天光雲影共徘徊。
問渠那得清如許，為有源頭活水來。

On Reading　　　　　　　　Zhu Xi

A square pond spreads
　like a mirror, over which
　　sky-light and shadows

of clouds are throwing
　patterns: an expanse of
　　intoxicating loveliness.

Why should the water be
　so clear and clean? Because
　　it has a running headspring.

凝　　　　　　　　　　　　林明理

這一畦稻浪
隨牛背上的炊煙飄來……

泊在水月裡

我想起幼時木麻黃下的鞦韆
螢火蟲躲閃著
到哪兒去？在風中踏響
那步履兒
可是踽踽而行的母親
而不安的亮星
於山村的木橋上
多了些牽掛

Gaze　　　　　　　　　　　　　　　　　　Lin Ming-Li

This rice field
Coming with the smoke from the cattle backs……

Parked in the water moon
I think of the swing under the casuarinas when I was a child
Fireflies dodge
Where to go? Treading in the wind
That move
But the walking mother
And the restless bright star
On the wooden bridge in the mountain village
More worries

3·

題榴花　　　　　　　　　　　　　　　　　　朱熹

五月榴花照眼明，枝間時見子初成。
可憐此地無車馬，顛倒蒼苔落絳英。

To Pomegranate Flowers Zhu Xi

The pomegranate flowers
 in June are dazzlingly
  bright; branches and

twigs reveal fruits which
 are freshly ripe. There
  are no vehicles running

here, hence a loveable
 scene: crimson pomegranate
  flowers pile on green moss.

夏至清晨 林明理

哼著山歌的稻花上
坐著一隻介蟲殼兒，戲水
飛空——影子拖曳著影子
四面屏風
從跟前遛過

我擺脫了山後陰影
像綠光裏的羊
把腳步放慢
一條彎路連接無盡
水裡的雲追趕著月亮

The Morning of Summer Solstice
Lin Ming-Li

On the rice blossom humming with mountain songs
A cypris is sitting, playing with water

Flying in the sky — a shadow pulling another shadow
Screens from the four sides
Slide past before the eyes

I have cast off the shadow behind the mountain
Like the lamb in the green light
To slow down steps
A circuitous road is endless
The clouds in water are pursuing the moon

4 ·

元日   王安石

爆竹聲中一歲除,春風送暖入屠蘇。
千門萬戶曈曈日,總把新桃換舊符。

The Spring Festival   Wang Anshi

The noise of firecrackers
　　packs off an old year;
　　　　in warm spring wind

people are drinking wine.
　　A new sun is shining
　　　　on doors after doors,

when the old peach wood
　　is replaced by a new one,
　　　　to exorcise evil spirits.

在白色的森林下面　　　　　　　　林明理

在白色的森林下面
我聽遠方細微的聲
從海峽吹來的風
　　　　默默無言地
在小徑裡面藏身
啊，我願跟著你
放鬆片刻
讓世界保持圓型吧
　　圓得似你無邪的瞳孔
而我所知道的名字
就寫在今年的耶誕夜密葉上

Under the White Forest　　　　　Lin Ming-Li

Under the white forest
I hear the subtle voice from afar
Breeze from the Straits
　　　　Silent
Hiding inside the trail
Ah, I will follow you
To relax for a moment
Let the world stay round
　　　Round as your innocent pupils
And I know the name
Written on the leaves of this year's Christmas Eve

宋詩明理接千載
古今抒情詩三百首
漢英對照

5.

梅花   王安石

牆角數枝梅，凌寒獨自開。
遙知不是雪，為有暗香來。

Plum Blossoms   Wang Anshi

A few plum blossoms
  are blooming solitarily,
    in the wall corner,

against the cold current.
  They are known to
    be no snow from afar:

there is an overflowing
  of flowery fragrance
    hither and thither.

冬之戀   林明理

掠過花溪的櫻之影
波光盪漾的山之音
周圍在歡唱，在漫舞，
而我感到幸福的是
那微雨中慢坡的小路，
那影樹交錯中的粉紅
——像個花仙子
  在香階的霧中……

The Love of Winter　　　　Lin Ming-Li

The shadow of cherry blossoms flitting across the flowery creek
The mountain voice rippling and poppling with waves
All about there is merry singing and joyful dancing
What makes me happy is
The gently sloped road in a drizzle
The pink interspersed with shadows of trees
— Like a Flower Faerie
　　In the fog with scented steps······

泊船瓜州　　　　王安石

京口瓜洲一水間，鐘山只隔數重山。
春風又綠江南岸，明月何時照我還？

Anchor My Boat at Guazhou　　Wang Anshi

Jingkou and Guazhou
　　are separated by a river;
　　　　Zhongshan is only

several green hills away.
　　The spring wind again
　　　　has greened the Southern

Shore; bright moon, when
　　can you shine on me
　　　　along my homeward way?

在那星星上 　　　　　　　　　　林明理

我望著花間雨露
像布穀鳥，掠過
潺潺的小河，而搖曳
在稻浪的，春之舞

Over the Stars 　　　　　　　Lin Ming-Li

I gaze at dewdrops among the flowers
Like a cuckoo bird, flitting
Past the gurgling river, swaying
In the waves of paddy field, the dance of spring

---

7 ·

書湖陰先生壁 　　　　　　　　王安石

茅簷長掃淨無苔，花木成畦手自栽。
一水護田將綠繞，兩山排闥送青來。

Written on the Wall of My Neighbor
　　　　　　　　　　　　　　　Wang Anshi

Swept from time to time,
　the courtyard of a thatched
　　hut is free of moss; lines

of trees and clumps of flowers
　are planted by the host
　　himself. A river nurtures

the cropland: lush and green.
　A wicket appears between
　　two hills: green is brought in.

靜寂的黃昏　　　　　　　　　　　林明理

一隻秋鷺立著，牠望著遠方。
萋萋的蘆葦上一葉扁舟。
對岸：羊咩聲，鼓噪四周的蛙鳴。
牠輕輕地振翅飛走，
羽毛散落苗田，
彷彿幾絲村舍的炊煙。

Silent Dusk　　　　　　　　　　Lin Ming-Li

An autumn heron stands, looking into the distance.
There is a small boat floating on lush reeds.
The opposite bank: sheep bleating, frogs croaking all around.
Gently flapping its wings, it flies away,
Feathers scattered in the seedling fields,
Like a few wisps of cottage kitchen smoke.

登飛來峰　　　　　　　　　　　王安石

飛來峰上千尋塔，聞說雞鳴見日升。
不畏浮雲遮望眼，自緣身在最高層。

The Peak of Flight Wang Anshi

Atop the Peak of Flight,
    there is a cloud-kissing ancient
        pagoda; it is said a climber

at the crow of the rooster to
    the great height can admire
        the sunrise. I do not fear the

scurrying clouds obstruct my
    view, because I find myself on
        the topmost floor of the tower.

寂靜的遠山 林明理

寂靜的遠山
夜鶯，枝椏，落葉掃著水面
我以詩
    漫射出甜美的語言
歌唱比微笑更顯著的夜空
那細微的鈴聲，隱隱傳來
    ——是牧羊人回家了

The Silent Remote Mountain Lin Ming-Li

The silent remote mountain
Nightingales, branches, falling leaves kissing water
With poetry
    I diffuse sweet words
The night sky where singing is louder than smiles
The subtle bell, travels here faintly
    — The shepherd is back home

9．

遊鐘山　　　　　　　　　　　王安石

終日看山不厭山，買山終待老山間。
山花落盡山長在，山水空流山自閑。

Touring the Bell Mountain　　Wang Anshi

Daylong looking at the Bell Mountain,
   without a touch of tedium in the heart,
     and I buy a plot in the mountain

for my future tomb. Mountain
   flowers blossom and fade and fall,
     one and all, yet green mountains

stay; the creek water is running
   vainly by itself, and the Bell Mountain
     is still leisurely and carefree.

致青山　　　　　　　　　　　林明理

我昂首
   如伸向天空的長頸鹿，
千朵萬朵雲兒掠過，
從綠油油的谷地到無邊的海角。
古老的土地上已沒有任何喧囂……
在這裡，
時間靜止不動，
   月朦朧，鳥棲息。

To the Green Mountain Lin Ming-Li

I raise my head
    Like a giraffe stretching its neck skyward,
Thousands of clouds sail by,
From the greenish valley to the boundless cape.
The age-old land is free from any noise….
Here
Time stands still;
    The moon is moony, birds at rest.

---

10 ·

江上 王安石

江北秋陰一半開，晚雲含雨卻低徊。
青山繚繞疑無路，忽見千帆隱映來。

On the River Wang Anshi

Autumn clouds in the sky north of the
    river: half blotting out the sky and the
        sun, and half scattering; the murky clouds

at dusk hang and hover low, threatening
    rain. A distant view: a cluster after another
        cluster of blue mountains are steaming

with mist and clouds, seemingly no
    thoroughfare, when thousands of sails
        loom all of a sudden, from nowhere.

季雨來了   林明理

所有島嶼不約而同地發聲
所有生物都在唱和──
在婆羅洲[1]熱帶雨林中,
如你有雙好眼睛
　　又能聽見魚群的舞蹈
豬籠草的捕誘,樹鼩的竊笑
　　海龜也在漫遊著...
啊,我是我命運的主宰
我做我想要的
　　──自由和冒險;
而感受大自然的美妙也將
　　隨之而來。

The Rainy Season Is Coming   Lin Ming-Li

Spontaneously all islands make the voice
All creatures sing in chorus —
In the tropical rainforest of Borneo[2],
If you have a pair of clairvoyant eyes
　　And can hear the dancing fishes
The trapping Nepenthes, the snickering of tree shrews
　　The sea turtles are also roaming ....
Ah, I am the master of my destiny
I do what I want to do
— Freedom and adventurous;
And the feeling of natural beauty
　　Will follow suit.

---

[1] 婆羅洲(馬來語:Borneo),是世界第三大島,亞洲第一大島。
[2] Borneo (Malay: Borneo) is the third largest island in the world and the largest island in Asia.

11.

鐘山即事　　　　　　　　　　　　王安石

澗水無聲繞竹流，竹西花草弄春柔。
茅簷相對坐終日，一鳥不鳴山更幽。

Life in the Bell Mountain　　　Wang Anshi

Creek water encircles the bamboo
　　grove, running voicelessly; flowers
　　　　and grass west of the grove are

tenderly gentle in the spring breeze.
　　Daylong sitting under the eaves of
　　　　a thatched cottage which is lost in

brown study of beautiful scenery, I feel
　　the reigning quietness in the mountain
　　　　without a single twitter of birds.

山的呢喃　　　　　　　　　　　　林明理

噢赫莫薩
　　神的最深顧盼
如天使的一滴淚
　　滴落地面般
我是一個守護者
　　在閃耀的天地之間
聆聽樹林交響

而你靜靜晃動的眼神
既深且藍
　不曾改變模樣

Whisper of the Mountain　　　Lin Ming-Li

Oh Hermosa
　God's deepest concern
Like a teardrop of the angel
　falling onto the ground
I am a guardian
　Between the shining heaven and earth
Listening to the woods' symphony
And you wordlessly roll your eyes
Deep and blue
　Without any change

夜吟　　　　　　　　　　　　　　陸遊

六十餘年妄學詩，功夫深處獨心知。
夜來一笑寒燈下，始是金丹換骨時。

Composing Poems in the Depth of Night　　　Lu You

Infatuated with poetry for over
　sixty years, my consummate
　　writing skills are privy to none.

Under a cold lamp in such
   a cold night, I smile to myself,
     glorying in my own poems.

夜之聲 林明理

夜深
雨落柿子樹上
秋天瞇著眼
編織角落小貓的夢

起初,我跟我的側影
互相參差唱和
一團寒風也忘了
滑過長街盡頭

而後,我輕輕一縱
像水鹿
諦聽
雪白而寧靜的湖色

Sound of the Night Lin Ming-Li

Late into the night
Raindrops drop on the persimmon tree
Autumn squints its eyes
To weave a dream of the little cat in the corner

At first, my silhouette and I
Intermingle in harmony with each other
A spell of cold wind forgets
To slide across the end of the long street

Then, gently I stretch
Like a water deer
To listen to
The snow-white and still lake

13 ·

示兒 陸遊

死去原知萬事空，但悲不見九州同。
王師北定中原日，家祭無忘告乃翁。

My Will to My Son Lu You

Upon dying, I know that everything
   turns empty; I can hardly contain myself
      for sorrow: the nine states of China

have not been unified. This brings
   my mind back to the nagging worry
      which has been my constant companion

for the greater part of my lifetime.
   When the imperial army has eventually
      recovered the north land, forget not,

in family sacrifice, to tell your father
   this news in the nether world, which
      will be a great cause of joy to me.

我哭，在西牆 林明理

讓我做夢吧
　　　　我哭，在西牆[3]
那來自天空的祈禱聲
低低切切，吹遍聖殿山與河谷
我將你的愛寫在地中海的群星上
　　　恰似水藍色的風
悄悄滑過每段歷史與愛的
　　　縐摺之痛

I Weep Against the West Wall Lin Ming-Li

Let me dream a dream
　　　I weep against the west wall[4]
The prayer from the sky
Low and lowly, blow across temples and valleys
I write your love on the stars of the Mediterranean
　　　Just like the water-blue wind
Stealthily sliding over the crumpled pain
　　　Of each episode of history and love

---

[3] 傳說第二聖殿被催毀時，有天使在西牆上哭泣，後來只有這段 18 米的殘垣斷壁留存下來，因而西牆又稱哭牆。

[4] Legend has it that when the second temple was destroyed, there were angels crying on the western wall, with this 18-meter ruins left behind, hence the western wall is also called the weeping wall.

14 ·

冬夜讀書示子聿   陸遊

古人學問無遺力，少壯工夫老始成。
紙上得來終覺淺，絕知此事要躬行。

To My Son When Reading in a Winter Night
       Lu You

The ancients spare no efforts
    in their scholarship: labor in early
       years, achievements in old age.

Book knowledge is shallow
    — until it is practiced in practice.

冬之歌   林明理

月光漫過草的山巔
積雪覆蓋石頭和溪流
此刻，星空覆蓋的多洛米蒂[5]
散發純淨的光
讓我內心無比地平和

Winter Song   Lin Ming-Li

Moonlight flows across the grassy mountaintop
Accumulated snow covers stones and streams

---

[5] 義大利北邊多洛米蒂（The Dolomites）在 2009 年被列入世界自然遺產。

Now, the Dolomites[6] covered with the sky
Emits pure light
Which renders my heart in great peace

---

15 ·

劍門道中遇微雨   陸遊

衣上征塵雜酒痕，遠遊無處不消魂。
此身合是詩人未？細雨騎驢入劍門。

Caught in a Drizzle on the Way   Lu You

Weary and travel-worn from
  a good bit of a journey made
    today, I am in a bad state of

my clothes, which are soiled
  with dust and stains of wine;
    yet travelling faraway, to any

place, is ravishing. Self-reflection:
  am I equal to the name of a poet?
    Riding a donkey, I, drenched

in the drizzling rain, enter
  the Sword Gate Pass, the
    greatest pass in the world.

---

[6] The Dolomites, a mountain range in the north of Italy, was listed as one of the World Natural Heritage Sites in 2009.

十月秋雨　　　　　　　　　　林明理

我記得你凝視的眼神。
你一頭微捲的褐髮，思維沉靜。
微弱的風拖在樹梢張望，
落葉在我腳底輕微地喧嚷。

你牽著我的手在畫圓，卻選擇兩平線：
銀河的一邊、數彎的濃霧、飛疾的電光，
那是我無法掌握前進的歸向，
我驚散的靈魂潛入了無明。

在山頂望夜空。從鐵塔遠眺到田野。
你的距離是無間、是無盡、是回到原點！
曉色的樺樹在你眼底深處雄立。
秋天的雨點在你身後串成連珠……

Autumn Rain of October　　　Lin Ming-Li

I remember your gaze.
Your crown of brown curls, your quiet thoughts.
The weak wind lingering atop the trees,
The fallen leaves rustling beneath my feet.

You take me by the hand to draw a circle while choosing two parallel lines:
By the Milky Way, the fog over several bays, sheets of lightning,
I fail to keep the direction of movement,
My startled soul dives into the bottomless dark.

Looking into the night sky atop the mountain, from the iron tower to the field.

The distance between you is no distance, endlessness, back
to the original point!
The morning birch is deeply rooted before your eyes.
The raindrops of autumn string into beads behind you....

---

16 ·

秋懷　　　　　　　　　　　　　　　　　　陸遊

園丁傍架摘黃瓜，村女沿籬采碧花。
城市尚餘三伏熱，秋光先到野人家。

A Tinge of Emotion at Autumn　　Lu You

The vegetable grower is standing
　against stands to pick cucumber,
　　when village girls are gathering

flowers from among green masses
　of hedge-side grass. Dog days
　　linger doggedly in cities, while

the countryside is already
　glowing with autumn tints.

秋的懷念　　　　　　　　　　　　　　　　林明理

秋近了，那片蘆花
　像一隻隻飛禽出沒
槳聲和蟲鳴在黃昏的湖中回轉

耳邊響起的，仍是那支歌
只有風和盤旋的燕
　　混唱著。而我曳著船
在風中寫你的名字
它輕輕划過……
　　在輕揚的水面上

The Fond Memory of Autumn　Lin Ming-Li

Autumn is around the corner, the patch of reed catkins
　　Seems to be infested with one after another bird
The oars and insects chirping are echoing over the dusk-veiled lake
　　The ears are ringing, still with the song
Only the wind and the wheeling swallow
　　Are singing together. I drag and pull the boat
To write your name in the wind
It gently flashes past……
　　On the gently waving surface

17・

十一月四日風雨大作　　　　　　　　陸遊

僵臥孤村不自哀，尚思為國戍輪台。
夜闌臥聽風吹雨，鐵馬冰河入夢來。

Composed in a Rainstorm

Lu You

Bedridden in the lonely bed
   of a lonely mountain village,
      I harbor no self-pity, yearning

to garrison frontiers of my mother-
   land. At dead of night I lend an ear
      to the stormy wind caught in rain,

before the sound of armored horse
   hooves coming up icebound rivers
      travels to the margin of my dream.

重複的雨天

林明理

曾經
我遇上一個無羈人，
他就像一隻長長的風箏
直想飛越沙漠和大洋，
孤單地朝向夢想，
而我
隔著層層白雲，
不再探問風兒、彩虹和駭浪，
不再想起輕吻的瞬間，
就像這無聲息地
重複的雨天。

那雨聲淅瀝——
風凝固在宿舍前。
晚上十點鐘。
接著路燈黯淡了，
我只看見桌上留下

一朵啞默的玫瑰,
在黑暗中
　悄悄地閃現,
就好像當我回頭瞥見,
一把藍綠小傘,遮掩了
懸在半空中的淚。

Rainy Days Which Repeat Themselves
　　　　　　　　　　　Lin Ming-Li

Once
I met an undisciplined man,
Who is like a long kite
Intending to fly across the desert and ocean,
Alone toward the dream,
When I
Partitioned by layers of white clouds,
No longer care about the wind, rainbow,
or frightening waves,
No longer recall to mind the moment of gentle kiss,
Like these wordless
Rainy days which repeat themselves.

The rain is rustling: —
The wind frozen before the dormitory.
Ten o'clock at night.
And the street lights begin to dim,
I only see on the table
There is a mute rose,
In darkness
　Quietly flashing,
Seemingly when I glance back,
To see a small blue & green umbrella, to cover
The tears hanging in mid-air.

18 ·

沈園二首（其一）　　　　　　　　　　陸遊

城上斜陽畫角哀，沈園非復舊池台。
傷心橋下春波綠，曾是驚鴻照影來。

Two Poems Composed in Shen Garden: for My Former Wife (1)　Lu You

From the city wall bathed
　in the slanting sun, the bugle
　　sounds melancholy and doleful;

Shen Garden is beautiful no
　more: it is dilapidated and desolate.
　　More heartbreaking is that the

pool of spring water under the
　small bridge has ever mirrored
　　her form of stunning beauty.

晚秋　　　　　　　　　　　　　　　　林明理

在一片濃綠的陡坡
白光之下和風，把高地淅淅吹著。
妳回首望，淡淡的長裙
弄散滿地丁香。

我看見
花瓣掉落山城垂楊
晨霧漸失。雲雀
驚動了松果，妳淺淺一笑
彷彿世界揚起了一陣笙歌，
而笙歌在妳的四周
有無法不感到讚嘆的奇趣。

今夜，
月已悄默，
只要用心端詳
石階草露也凝重
妳離去的背影催我斷腸
就像秋葉搖搖欲墜
又怎抵擋得住急驟的風？

Late Autumn   Lin Ming-Li

On a steep slope heavy with green
Under the white light, the breeze is blowing over the highland.
Looking back, you see a pale long skirt
Which scatters lilac scent all over the ground.

I see
Petals falling from the weeping willows in the mountain city
The morning mist gradually disappears. Skylarks
Startle the pine cones; you wanly smile
As if the world is noisy with singing,
Which is around you
There is a wonder which cannot be allayed.

Tonight,
The moon is silent,
As long as you look carefully
The stone steps are moist with dew
Your retreating form renders me heartbroken
Like autumn leaves on the falling
How to resist the strong wind?

19．

沈園二首（其二） 陸遊

夢斷香消四十年，沈園柳老不吹綿。
此身行作稽山土，猶吊遺蹤一泫然。

Two Poems Composed in Shen Garden: for My Former Wife (2) Lu You

The dream, shattered; the scent,
   vanished — an elapse of forty years;
     once more to the garden, I find the

willow tree too old to produce catkins.
   I'm on the verge of turning into a
     handful of soil beneath Huiji Mountain

and, at the sight of your traces here
   in the former days, still I cannot
     help shedding my hot tears on tears.

寒夜的奇想   林明理

當午夜狂雪遠逸,
覆蓋楓樹的光澤
與甜夢,風不再咆嘯,
只有回憶帶著我繼續飄翔,
引我期待些什麼。

當愛輕叩窗欞的時候,
它就像上天的賜福,
崇高而美好,
像突如其來的吻,
驚喜卻毫不做作。

我根本不想理解,
它為什麼總是來去無蹤?
因為,當愛歸來的時候,
它就像涓涓不息的小河,
你可以選擇追隨,——

卻無法改變它原有的渠道,
而我很清楚,
愛,有時像鴿子,
那咕咕聲,來自喜悅,
來自遠方迢遙的窗口。

Cold Night Fantasy   Lin Ming-Li

When the midnight snow flies far away,
Covered is the sheen of the maple trees
And the sweet dream; the wind howls no more,
And only memories take me in the continuous flight,
Leading me into some expectation.

When love taps on the window sills,
It is like a blessing from heaven,
Sublime and beautiful,
Like a sudden kiss,
Surprising and unpretentious.

I don't want to understand it,
Why does it always come and go without a trace?
For, when love returns,
It is like a babbling river.
You can choose to follow it —

But its original channel cannot be changed,
And I know it very well.
Love, sometimes like a dove,
The cooing, out of joy,
From a dim and distant window.

---

20 ·

春思   方嶽

春風多可太忙生，長共花邊柳外行。
與燕作泥蜂釀蜜，才吹小雨又須晴。

Spring Wind   Fang Yue

Spring wind is a busybody — she
　blows flowers into blossoming,
　　and she blows willows into greening;

she makes the earth warm again:
　　　　she melts the mud for swallows
　　　　　　to make nests and helps the bees

　　to make honey by opening the
　　　　flowery petals for them; she brings
　　　　　　a mass of dark clouds which produce

　　a shower of rain, and she blows
　　　　away the dark clouds to exhibit
　　　　　　a sky which is clean and clear.

春雪──致吾友張智中教授[7]　　　　林明理

1.
在遠方,那雪景我窺視激越,
它遮蔽彩虹和天梯的距離,恰似
白羽的孔雀,二月的春雪。

2.
昨夜,當大地睡熟了。
雪原就飛入你詩意的眼睛,還是
那樣使人目不轉睛,一切未變。

3.
我會記住,在格調松間的高樓裡,
雪花唱著穿過了大學校園;
以及你眼裡的溫存……

---

[7] 任教於南開大學外語系博士班導師的友人張智中教授於今晨傳來一張其住處的窗景。他是位博學多聞又熱愛詩歌的學者,有幸與他合著《詩林明理──古今抒情詩160首》,遂而有感而詩。
　——2024.02.21 寫於台灣

4.
噢，春雪，你是夢幻的雲朵，
任誰也譜不出你的清音和笑意，
如同為你祝福的星辰。

Spring Snow — To My Friend Professor Zhang Zhizhong[8]   Lin Ming-Li

1.
In the distance, I peer at the snowy scene in excitement;
It covers the distance between rainbow and heavenly ladder, just like
The white-feathered peacock, spring snow in February.

2.
Last night, when the great earth is sound asleep,
The snowfield flies into your poetic eye, still
Fixing the eye to it, nothing changed.

3.
I will remember, in the tall building of the Elegant Pines Residence,
Snowflakes are singing and dancing through the university campus,
As well as the tenderness in your eyes······

---

[8] My friend Professor Zhang Zhizhong, who teaches as a doctoral supervisor in the Translation Department of the School of Foreign Studies, Nankai University, sent me a photo freshly taken through his window this morning. He is an erudite scholar and a great lover of poetry, with whom I have the honor to co-author Parallel Reading of 160 Ancient and Modern Chinese Lyrical Poems (Chinese-English), hence this poem. (February 21, 2024; Taiwan)

4.
Oh, spring snow, you are the dreamy clouds;
Nobody can interpret your crisp voice and gentle smile,
Like the stars blessing you.

---

21 •

農謠五首（其一） 方嶽

春雨初晴水拍堤，村南村北鵓鴣啼。
含風宿麥青相接，刺水柔秧綠未齊。

Ballads (No. 1 of 5 poems) Fang Yue

A shiny day after a spring
   rain, the river water is lapping
     against the bank; the north and

south of the village are noisy
   with the twitters of wood pigeons.
     The wheat sown every other

year is undulating with a stretch
   of dark green upon another
     stretch of dark green; the

tender sprouts just growing
   out of water, with various
     heights, are unevenly green.

海波親吻了向晚的霞光

林明理

1.
風兒沉默。我心悵然,
海波親吻向晚的雲影,
我親吻你心底的憂傷。

2.
噢,朋友,人生只一回,
何不滿懷希望,
諦聽星空天使的合唱?

3.
主啊,我慶幸能生活於平靜,
為讚頌袮,我願對著宇宙,
向靜海歌詠。

The Waves Kiss the Evening Glow

Lin Ming-Li

1.
The wind is silent. I am saddened,
The sea waves kiss the shadows of evening clouds,
When I kiss the sadness in your heart.

2.
Oh, dear friend, we all live once,
Why not let our life be filled with hopes
To listen to the chorus of angels in the starry sky?

3.
Lord, I am blessed to live in peace,
To praise you, I would like to sing to the silent sea,
Against the vast universe.

22

江上   劉子翬

江上潮來浪薄天，隔江寒樹晚生煙。
北風三日無人渡，寂寞沙頭一簇船。

On the Autumn River   Liu Zihui

With the surging sea tide, the breakers
    seem to break the sky; in the evening,
        the woods across the river is cold

with a thin film of rising mist.
    The northern gale blowing hard
        for days on end, the ferry is empty

of any soul; at the lonely end of
    the sand beach there is anchorage
        of a tuft of boats, tangled into a mass.

冬日的魔法   林明理

雪已融
    露出無樹荒野
世界有時在我身上開個玩笑
    而你，巨大的力量
觸及我的靈魂
    猶如溫暖陽光
讓北極大地生機盎然

The Magic of Winter   Lin Ming-Li

Snow has melted
>To reveal the wilderness without trees

The world occasionally makes fun of me

And you, a great power
>To touch my soul

Like the warm sunshine
>For the North Polar Region to be filled with life

---

23 •

汴京紀事二十首（其五）   劉子翬

梁園歌舞足風流，美酒如刀解斷愁。
憶得少年多樂事，夜深燈火上樊樓。

Twenty Poems about Reminiscences in the Capital of Bianjing (No. 5 of 20 poems)   Liu Zihui

Reminisce about the good old days:
>the imperial garden is constantly noisy
>>with singing and dancing, a dissolute

and debauched life. The liquor, like
>the blade of a knife, can cut off sorrow in
>>the heart. Youthful days see how many merry-

making occasions: the depth of night and
　　　a streetful of bright lamps, when I come to
　　　　the most famous merry mansion of the capital.

九份之夜　　　　　　　　　　　　　　　林明理

　　夜，黯然下來了
　每一個紅燈籠，都撩我
　　摩挲著往事
　自群星間到霧谷之中

　是誰說
　　酒是液體的火？
　在雨聲裡
　在時間裡
　在灰燼裡
　　我忽然想到：
　　一座昇平戲院如何連結兩個時空
　　又或許在那兒誰也不埋怨什麼

　　春風太早，躲藏在我的口袋裡
　你的影子剪於二月
　　前方有窗櫺相對在叮叮響起
　響著的名字也仍舊如是

The Night of Jiufen　　　　　　　　Lin Ming-Li

　　The night, begins to dim and dark
　Each red lantern is tantalizing to me
　　Recalling the past events
　From the maze of stars to the misty valley

67

Who says that
　　The wine is a liquid fire?
In the sound of rain
In the time
In the ashes
　　Suddenly I remember:
　　How can a peaceful theater connect two spaces
　　Or perhaps nobody complains about anything

　　The spring wind comes too early, to hide in my pocket
Your form is cut in February
　　In front the window lattices are jingling and　　tinkling
　　Still ringing with the old name

---

24 ·

遊園不值　　　　　　　　　　　　　　　葉紹翁

應憐屐齒印蒼苔，小扣柴扉久不開。
春色滿園關不住，一枝紅杏出牆來。

Failing to Meet a Friend　　　Ye Shaoweng

Afraid of my clogs crushing the
　　green sward? The wicket gate
　　　refuses to open in spite of my

persistent rapping, tapping, knocking……
　　The garden is exploding with growth,
　　　with color and scent: a gardenful

of spring is a gardenful of desire
　　— a petal-decked apricot branch,
　　　　over the wall, is swaying and flaming……

在山丘的彼方　　　　　　　　　　林明理

一種聲音
猶如棕雀，在斜暉脈脈時
響起——

狗尾草何以如此美麗
我信步在霧林
又有誰縈回夢裡？

那拖曳的愛情星辰
也曾一瞥
在漆黑四壁，柔聲絮語

On the Other Side of the Hill　Lin Ming-Li

A voice
Like a palm-colored sparrow, in the sun setting aslant
Is arising —

How can a green bristle grass be so beautiful
I ramble in the misty forest
Who is having a fond dream?

That star of love which is twinkling
Has ever cast a glance
Against the dark walls, is murmuring gently

25．

夜書所見　　　　　　　　　　　　　葉紹翁

蕭蕭梧葉送寒聲，江上秋風動客情。
知有兒童挑促織，夜深籬落一燈明。

View of an Autumn Night　　　Ye Shaoweng

A cold autumn gives rise to gusts
　　of speedy wind, blowing the leaves
　　　　of parasol trees into dancing; over

the river, the wind with a touch of
　　autumn most touches the wanderer
　　　　who, from afar, knows the children

are catching and playing crickets
　　by the side of the hedge, where
　　　　a lamp is flickering and twinkling.

細密的雨聲　　　　　　　　　　　　林明理

你在哪裡逗留？
－在雨中，穿過
時間的荊棘；

是什麼樣的愛情，
把你凝成
樹痂般的岩顏，
要你如此伏臥
不停震顫到另一個明天？

The Dense Rain

Lin Ming-Li

Where are you lingering?
— In the rain, through
The thorn of time;

What kind of love
Has curdled you
Into a rock which is like the tree scab
For you to bend and lie down
On the shivering to another tomorrow?

雪梅

盧梅坡

梅雪爭春未肯降，騷人擱筆費評章。
梅須遜雪三分白，雪卻輸梅一段香。

Mume Flowers & Snowy Blossoms

Lu Meipo

The first sign of early spring:
    mume flowers, or snowy blossoms?
        Still an open question, when

the poet is a clumsy judge.
    Mume flowers are inferior
        to snowy blossoms in a stretch

of white; snowy blossoms are
　　inferior to mume flowers
　　　　in a measure of fragrance.

北京湖畔遐思[9]　　　　　　　　　林明理

光的藏匿處
那片樹林前方的
薄冰層上
我所看到的是
陌生又熟悉——
美麗的雁鴨
翔集於此
在濕地的晨光中
似乎應和著什麼

沿著湖畔
風　盡情馳騁
在那兒前進著
而我卻感到如此溫暖
彷若　一顆心
徜徉在北國
與雪花一起掠過的
還有我所寄予
厚重的盼望

---

[9] 來自北京大學秦立彥教授捎來信息及拍攝的野鴨照片，因而題詩留念。

Fantasy by the Lake of Beijing[10]

Lin Ming-Li

The place to hide the light
On the thin ice
Before the woods
What comes into my sight
Both strange and familiar —
The beautiful wild ducks
Gathering and frolicking here
In the morning light of the wetland
Seemingly to be echoing to something

Along the lake
The wind is speeding
Freely forward
And I feel so warm
As if a heart
Is wandering in the Northern Country
What is flying with snowflakes
Is my
Earnest hope

27 •

夏意

蘇舜欽

別院深深夏席清，石榴開遍透簾明。
樹陰滿地日當午，夢覺流鶯時一聲。

---

[10] The poem is inspired upon receiving a letter with photos of wild ducks from Qin Liyan, a professor of Peking University.

The Height of Summer   Su Shunqin

The deep yard is dotted
>with a bamboo mat which
>>is clear and cool; the curtain

is crystal bright with raging
>pomegranate blossoms. The
>>high noon sees the ground

dappled in light and shade,
>when the dream is punctuated by
>>the intermittent twitters of orioles.

塞哥維亞舊城[11]   林明理

一座孤獨的城堡
   恰似
      隨風盪漾的船
   靜靜睡在山崖上
只在夢中，回到中世紀的向晚
雲不曾改變過什麼
   群聚的星辰仍宴飲著
  這一季迷人的月色

The Old Town of Segovia[12]   Lin Ming-Li

A solitary castle
>Is like

---

[11] 西班牙的塞哥維亞（Segovia）舊城，雄踞在一個狹長的山岩上，被列為世界文化遺產。

[12] Segovia, as an old city of Spain, is located in a long and narrow stretch of rocky area, and is ranked as a world cultural heritage.

A boat waving in the wind
Sleeping quietly on the cliff
Only in a dream, back to the medieval evening
The cloud has changed nothing
The crowd of stars are still feasting
On the season of charming moon

28 ·

淮中晚泊犢頭　　　　　　　　蘇舜欽

春陰垂野草青青，時有幽花一樹明。
晚泊孤舟古祠下，滿川風雨看潮生。

Mooring in the Evening at Riverside Dutou
Su Shunqin

Spring, the overcast sky hanging low;
　it threatens winds & rains, when bankside
　　grass is lushly green; occasionally visible:

a treeful of flowers riotous with various
　colors in a secluded place, flare to be fair.
　　Dusk finds a lonely boat mooring by an

ancient temple, which is watching a river-
　ful of blowing winds and pelting rains,
　　while tide water is rushing and arising.

遠方的思念 　　　　　　　　　　　林明理

我想寄給你，寫在潔淨的
白雲輕靈的翅膀上
在這不是飄雪紛飛的冬天

我想寄給你
豪邁而無形式的歌
以及充滿友情的琴聲

雖然祝福在心中，天涯太遙遠
當你的眼睛逮住這朵雲
你將懂得我唱出的秘密

Yearning From Afar 　　　　　　Lin Ming-Li

I'd like to send it to you, written
On the light wings of pure clouds
On the winter without winnowing snow

I'd like to send it to you
An unrestrained formless song
As well as the luting charged with friendship

Though with blessing in heart, the sky is far away
When your eyes catch this blossom of cloud
You'll be privy to the secret of my singing

29·

和淮上遇便風 　　　　　　　　　　　蘇舜欽

浩蕩清淮天共流,長風萬裡送歸舟。
應愁晚泊喧卑地,吹入滄溟始自由。

Sailing on Huaihe River in the Tail Wind
Su Shunqin

The river water is limpid and mighty,
　　rushing and rolling into the horizon;
　　　　the wind blows as long as ten thousand

miles, accompanying a leaf of returning
　　boat. Sorrowful: at eventide, a boat is
　　　　mooring in a place which is low, wet,

and noisy; a better choice: go downstream
　　into the boundless sea, for real freedom.

四月的夜風 　　　　　　　　　　　林明理

悠悠地,略過松梢
充滿甜眠和光,把地土慢慢甦復
光浮漾起海的蒼冥
我踱著步。水聲如雷似的
切斷夜的偷襲

我聽見
野鳩輕輕地低喚,與
唧唧的蟲兒密約

古藤下,我開始想起
去年春天。你側著頭
回眸望一回,你是凝,是碧翠
是一莖清而不寒的睡蓮!

這時刻,林裡。林外
星子不再窺視於南窗
而我豁然瞭解:
曾經有絲絲的雨,水波拍岸
在踩石山前的路上……

The Night Wind of April Lin Ming-Li

Passes, lazily, over the tops of pine trees
Filled with fond sleep and light, gently to waken the land
The light is rippling with the sea's dark green
I am strolling. The water sounds as thunders
To cut off the sneak attack of the night

I hear
Wild ducks gently cooing, and
Tryst with the chirping insects
Under old vines, I begin to recall
The last spring. You keep your head aslant
Backward glance, you are the condensation, emerald green
A stem of pond lily which is pure and free of cold!

Now, in the woods. Beyond the woods
The stars peer into the southern window no more
And I am suddenly enlightened:
There have been drizzling rain, waves lapping against the shore
On the road before the mountain of quarry……

30・

微涼　　　　　　　　　　　　　　　　　　寇准

高桐深密間幽篁，乳燕聲稀夏日長。
獨坐水亭風滿袖，世間清景是微涼。

Slight Cool　　　　　　　　　　　　　Kou Zhun

A dense bamboo grove, penetrative and
　　profound, is intermingled with towering
　　　　phoenix trees; thickening and darkening
as summer advances into its height, the
　　grove is a muffler of the chirping of young
　　　　swallows. Sitting alone in the wind-blown

water-side pavilion, I feel my sleeves
　　keep fluttering in the breeze, when a slight
　　　　cool brings pure scene to human world.

馬丘比丘之頌[13]　　　　　　　　　　　　林明理

我看見一隻老鷹徜徉於雲霧之中
這神廟即使是廢墟，也還是美的
加上那印弟安酋長的山巔之像
正聆聽遠方信號……它永不遺忘
來自星宿的各種訊息——從輝煌的
印加之城到現在的太陽塔日升之處

---

[13] 馬丘比丘 Machu Picchu 位於秘魯，是印加帝國（Incan Empire）的遺蹟。這座古城坐落於海拔 2,430 公尺的山脊上，地勢險要，有著「天空之城」及「失落的印加城市」之稱。它是世界新七大奇蹟之一，1983 年被列為世界遺產保護區。與此同時，馬丘比丘也面臨著遭旅遊業破壞的擔憂。

Ode to Machu Picchu[14]   Lin Ming-Li

I see an old eagle wheeling in the clouds
The temple is ruins, which is beautiful
And the statue of the Indian Chief atop the mountain
Is listening to the signal from afar….it never has lapse of memory
Various messages from the constellation — from the splendid
Incan City to the present Sun Tower where the run rises

31·

夏日   寇准

離心杳杳思遲遲，深院無人柳自垂。
日暮長廊聞燕語，輕寒微雨麥秋時。

The Early Summer   Kou Zhun

The parting sorrows are nowhere
   to be seen, and sluggish is my train
      of thought; deep is the courtyard,

---

[14] Machu Picchu, as the relic of the Incan Empire, is located on the mountain crest with an elevation of 2,430 meters in Peru. The terrain is strategically situated and hard of access, hence the name of "a city in the sky" and "the lost Incan City". It is listed among the new seven wonders of the world and, in 1983 it was designated a NESCO World Heritage site. At the same time, there is worry about Machu Picchu being destroyed by tourism.

too deep to see a single soul —
   only willows are weeping and
      drooping. At eventide, the swallows

are twittering in the long corridor,
   when the wheat is ripening, after
      a rainfall which brings light cold.

黃昏   林明理

越過綠野和海洋
我找到夕陽最後深情地一閃
正如四月桐鑲著雲彩
隱蔽於坡谷之下

Dusk   Lin Ming-Li

Over the green field and across the ocean
I finally find the setting sun's final flash of affection
Just like the April parasol trees which are embroidered with clouds
Hidden in the slope of the valley

畫眉鳥   歐陽修

百囀千聲隨意移，山花紅紫樹高低。
始知鎖向金籠聽，不及林間自在啼。

The Blackbird   Ouyang Xiu

chirps and twitters as she pleases,
   in the mountain red and purple
      with flowers: some high, some low.

In the woods, the blackbird
   enjoys more freedom and ease
      than being locked in a golden cage.

這一夏夜   林明理

微風吹拂
穿過溪流
和山崗
而我興高采烈地
跟著奔跑
還輕吻了月

This Summer Night   Lin Ming-Li

A breeze blows
Across rivers and rills
And hills
Cheerfully I follow
In running along
While gently kissing the moon

33 •

別滁 　　　　　　　　　　　　　歐陽修

花光濃爛柳輕明，酌酒花前送我行。
我亦且如常日醉，莫教弦管作離聲。

Demoted to Chuzhou 　　　Ouyang Xiu

The flowers bloom fair
　and flourishing, willow twigs
　　gently waving; a banquet is

arranged among the flowers
　to see me off. I'm as drunk
　　as a lord, which is my way

of drinking; piping music is
　welcome, except the sentimental
　　notes of lingering parting.

霧起的時候 　　　　　　　　　林明理

我們不期而遇
原以為世上的一切都不孤寂
沒有客套寒暄
彷彿重逢是天經地義
然而
那熟悉的身影如晴雨
空漠地飄過在死亡中的廣場

霧正在升起
喧囂的人群　傘花晃動

宋詩明理搖千載
古今抒情詩三百首
漢英對照

街的盡頭　雨霧迷濛
空氣裏有著露珠的味道
一隻貓　蜷縮在樹底
似乎等待著什麼
久雨初霽後
十月的黃昏　風淡描而過

When the Fog Is Rising Up　　　Lin Ming-Li

Accidentally we meet
We have held the belief that nothing in the world is lonely
No conventional greetings no standing on ceremony
As if the meeting is perfectly justified
However
That familiar figure is like a fine rain
Which hollowly floats across the square of death

The fog is rising up
The noisy crowd with tossing umbrella flowers
The end of the street is misty with fog and rain
The air is moist with the taste of dewdrops
A cat　crouching under the tree
Seems to be waiting for something
It is fine from a wet season
Dusk in October, a breeze blows briskly

34．

豐樂亭遊春三首（其三）　　　歐陽修

紅樹青山日欲斜，長郊草色綠無涯。
遊人不管春將老，來往亭前踏落花。

Spring Excursion to the Pleasure Pavilion (No. 3 of 3 poems)   Ouyang Xiu

Red trees and green hills
　　see the sun slanting, and
　　　　the suburbs see green grass

stretching boundless. Spring
　　excursionists do not care
　　　　about spring on the wane:

they tread on fallen flowers
　　before the Pleasure Pavilion.

你的微笑是我的微風   林明理

今年嚴冬我們遙望遠方
談詩，相顧而笑
你說
你的微笑是我的微風
那想來就是最真的自然了
我要說你是唯一的而我正費思
想你恰似一小片海域
卻和廣闊的海洋相隔
是的，我們在溫和的沙灘上走
空氣中有海藻的味道

Your Smile Is a Breeze for Me   Lin Ming-Li

This severe winter we gaze afar
Talking about poetry, smiling to each other
You say
Your smile is a breeze for me

Which is thought to be the most genuine nature
I want to say that you are the only one in my thought
I am pining for you like a small patch of sea
Yet to be separated by a vast ocean
Yes, we are walking along the quiet beach
The air smells of seaweed

---

35 •

和梅聖俞杏花　　　　　　　　　　歐陽修

誰道梅花早？殘年豈是春。
何如豔風日，獨自占芳辰。

In Reply to Mei Yaochen About Apricot Flowers　　　Ouyang Xiu

Who says plum blossoms
　are the first bloomer? The
　　dusk of the year falls short

of a new spring. In fine days
　of genial sunshine, each flower
　　and tree seems to be trying

to outshine the rest in brilliance
　and beauty, when apricot flowers
　　are particularly eye-catching.

早櫻 　　　　　　　　　　　　　　　林明理

掠過花溪的櫻之影
波光盪漾的山之音
周圍在歡唱，在漫舞，
而我感到幸福的是
那微雨中慢坡的小路，
那影樹交錯中的粉紅
——像個花仙子
在香階的霧中

Early Cherry Blossoms 　　　　Lin Ming-Li

The shadows of cherry blossoms floating over the flowery stream
The rippling sound of the mountains
All around there are singing and dancing,
And what makes me happy
Is the path with a gentle slope in the drizzle,
The pink in the interlaced shadows of the trees
— Like a flower fairy
In the mist lingering over fragrant steps

夏日絕句 　　　　　　　　　　　　李清照

生當作人傑，死亦為鬼雄。
至今思項羽，不肯過江東。

A Quatrain Composed in Summer

Li Qingzhao

Alive, be a hero
  of heroes; dead,
    be a ghost of ghosts.

Xiang Yu is my idol,
  who did disdain to
    outlive his underlings.

在白色的夏季裡

林明理

白日變長
鐘錶習慣停在九點零一刻
在夜晚的寧靜中
我走向傳說
很久以前
玫瑰花的野坡上輕輕踱步
整個七月充滿憂鬱
靈魂是一座密林
風依然無休止地來
修復了我思想的安定

In the White Summer

Lin Ming-Li

The days are turning longer
The clock is used to stopping at a quarter past nine
In the quietude of the night
I walk towards the legend
Long long ago
Gently strolling along the wild slope covered with roses

The whole July is filled with gloom
The soul is a dense forest
The wind still blows continuously
To restore the stability of my mind

37．

偶成   李清照

十五年前花月底，相從曾賦賞花詩。
今看花月渾相似，安得情懷似往時？

A Random Piece   Li Qingzhao

Fifteen years ago, amidst
   flowers and in the moonlight,
      we keep company with each

other to tour the garden, and
   we compose poems to admire
      the flowers. Now the flowers

and the moon are the same as
   those of yore, but my frame of
      mind, for no reason, is different.

海上的中秋   林明理

新雨乍晴，
遠山不染纖塵，

竟映照一抹閃紅，
點亮在古剎楊樹上。

風柔柔，四野寂然
只有白浪無止無息
憑依暮鼓聲聲。

我在霧中走著，
想摭拾一串串星顆，
讓階前草露的微音
隨風而去；
在霜徑菊香裏，
也在明月外。

Mid-Autumn at the Sea　　　　Lin Ming-Li

It is fine from rain,
The distant mountain is free from any mote of dust,
Which mirrors a flashing red,
On and against the poplars in an old temple.

Tender is the wind, and silence reigns in the wildness
Only white waves on the rolling
Punctuated by the evening drums.

Walking through the fog,
Intending to pick up strings of stars,
For the whispers of dewy grass before the steps
To be gone with wind:
In the frosty path fragrant with chrysanthemums,
Also beyond the bright moon.

渡漢江 宋之問

嶺外音書斷，經冬複曆春。
近鄉情更怯，不敢問來人。

Crossing River Han Song Zhiwen

News cut off from beyond
   the mountain, all the year
     round, from winter to spring

and onward. My growing
   timidity gets the better of
     me, as I approach home:

I dare not inquire about
   anything from anybody.

炫目的綠色世界 林明理

大黑麥田，農場和馬房
從空曠到金色的海面
我無法一一盛裝
翩翩而來的春天
就像思鄉的弦懸在耳畔

The Dazzling Green World Lin Ming-Li

Wheat fields of heavy black, farms and stables
From the expanse to the golden sea

I cannot one by one dress them up gorgeously
Spring approaches trippingly
Like homesickness which is ringing in the ears

39.

贈劉景文　　　　　　　　　　　蘇軾

荷盡已無擎雨蓋，菊殘猶有傲霜枝。
一年好景君須記，正是橙黃橘綠時。

To My Friend Liu Jingwen　　　Su Shi

Lotus flowers have withered, one
   and all; even the rain-proof lotus
      leaves have dried up and shriveled.

Chrysanthemum flowers, fading and
   drooping, still brave icy cold with their
      stubborn stems. The most beautiful season

of the year, remember, is the period of the
   end of autumn and the beginning of winter:
      oranges golden and tangerines green.

岸畔之樹　　　　　　　　　　　林明理

在我憩息的地方
岸畔之樹
像潺潺小溪

流經大片花田般
圍繞著我奏樂
在寂靜的森林內輕響

呵，那水貂似的髮絲
──我難尋踪跡的女孩
依著風的手指
忽隱忽現
快速地
問訊而來

只一瞬間
黑瞳晶若夜雪
妳是海
你是樹心
不，不是，你是輕風吹拂的白罌粟
我的一切，繆斯無法增添你一分光彩

The Trees Along the Bank   Lin Ming-Li

In the place where I rest
The trees along the bank
Like rippling rills and rivers
Flowing through a vast expanse of flowery field
While playing music about me
To gently echo in the quiet woods

Oh, the mink-like hair
— My girl who is traceless
Following the fingers of the wind
Appearing and disappearing
Quickly
For an inquiry

In the blink of an eye
Your black pupils glitter like snow in the night
You are the sea
You are the heart of the tree
Oh, no, you are the white poppy blown in the breeze
You are everything that counts for me; Muse fails to add to your brilliance

---

40 ·

六月二十七日望湖樓醉書 蘇軾

黑雲翻墨未遮山，白雨跳珠亂入船。
卷地風來忽吹散，望湖樓下水如天。

Tipsy at Lake-view Pavilion Su Shi

An endless bed of grey moves over
   the sky and mountain, murky clouds
      churning like Chinese ink, which bring

sheets of rain that smudges the color and
   contours out of everything, yet a distant
      hill has not been completely screened

from view. White raindrops bounce like
   pearls, beating the boat. Gusts of earth-
      rolling wind scatter the clouds, and

the water of the West Lake, under the
   pavilion, stills and is one with the sky.

愛情似深邃的星空

林明理

當愛情展翅翩翩，
誰都看得出它的快樂
就像孩童活潑的舞蹈！
在每一個重逢的瞬間，
魔法也在那兒。

但我更羨慕，
愛情似深邃的星空……
又像春天，滿身花朵！
它有隻奇異的眼睛，
永遠飽含著憂愁。

Love Is Like the Profound Starry Sky

Lin Ming-Li

When love spreads its wings,
Everybody can see its joy
Like the light-hearted dancing of a child!
In each moment of reunion,
There is magic.

Yet I admire more,
Love is like the profound starry sky……
Again like spring, filled with flowers!
It has a strange eye,
Which is brimming with sorrow.

41 ·

中秋月　　　　　　　　　　　　　　　　蘇軾

暮雲收盡溢清寒，銀漢無聲轉玉盤。
此生此夜不長好，明月明年何處看？

The Mid-autumn Moon　　　　　　　Su Shi

Dusk approaching, the clouds are
dispersed gradually, crisp air is overflowing;
　　in the still sky a jade disc is wheeling.

Such a mid-autumn moon, in my lifetime,
　　is not a well-wisher; this bright moon
　　　of the next year, where will be its watcher?

秋的懷念　　　　　　　　　　　　　　　林明理

秋近了，那片蘆花
　　像一隻隻飛禽出沒
槳聲和蟲鳴在黃昏的湖中回轉
　　耳邊響起的，仍是那支歌
只有風和盤旋的燕
　　混唱著。而我曳著船
在風中寫你的名字
它輕輕划過…
　　在輕揚的水面上

The Memory of Autumn　　　　　Lin Ming-Li

Autumn is around the corner, the stretch of reed catkins
　　Appear and disappear like a pair after another pair of birds

The oars and insect chirping are whirling in the dusk-veiled lake
    Ringing in the ears, still the song
Only the wind and the wheeling swallows
    Are singing together. I drag at the boat
To write your name in the wind
Gently it passes over....
    On the rippling surface

42 •

題西林壁   蘇軾

橫看成嶺側成峰，遠近高低各不同。
不識廬山真面目，只緣身在此山中。

The True Aspect of Lushan Mountain
Su Shi

Viewed horizontally, it is a ridge;
  vertically, a peak. High and low,
    far and near, Lushan Mountain

varies according as the landscape
  is differently clothed — a pregnant
    reflection. Illusory is the true

aspect of the mountain, height
  over height, forest over forest,
    where we find ourselves.

森林之歌   林明理

濃密的樹林中
蝶群自成一區
在某個時辰
　　振翅而出
前往雨林產卵
或者在草葉間
飛逐嬉戲
週遭是美麗的湖景
　　泥土、松香和
樹蛙聲
而我所到之處
都會聽見輕柔的鳴曲
　　曲聲盡是欣喜──
啊，陽光，雨水
　　涓涓滴流，都是詩意

Song of the Forest   Lin Ming-Li

In the dense forest
Butterflies throng of their own
At a certain hour
　　They wing out
Into the rainforest to lay eggs
Or in the grass
They fly and frolic
All about is the beautiful lake
　　Soil, rosin and
Croaking of tree frogs
Wherever I go
I hear gentle songs

Filled with joy —
Ah, sunshine, rainwater
　　Dripping and dropping, all poetic

43 ·

飲湖上初晴後雨　　　　　　　　蘇軾

水光瀲灩晴方好，山色空濛雨亦奇。
欲把西湖比西子，淡妝濃抹總相宜。

The West Lake: Sunny or Rainy　　Su Shi

Sunny, the waves are dimpling
　　in the sunshine, all the air flashes
　　　　and sparkles; rainy, surrounding hills

are hazy and misty — a constantly
　　wonderful scene. The West Lake
　　　　can be compared to an ancient beauty,

whose beauty is in the eye of the
　　beholder: made-up light or heavy.

西子灣夕照　　　　　　　　　　林明理

你的影像在
礁石浪潮中，
風甜甜地吹，
引我的思緒

留駐於心的記憶；
我記得
平灘上的每一足跡，
像今夜星辰般溫暖。
而我又告別了夕陽，
在大片天際線之下。

Sunset Over the West Lake Bay

Lin Ming-Li

Your image is in the waves
among the reefs,
The wind blows sweetly
To stir my thoughts
To keep memory in the heart;
I still remember
Each footprint on the beach,
Warm like the stars of tonight.
And I again say goodbye to the setting sun,
Under the vast skyline.

44·

春宵 蘇軾

春宵一刻值千金，花有清香月有陰。
歌管樓臺聲細細，秋千院落夜沉沉。

A Spring Night

Su Shi

An inch of spring night,
   an inch of gold; flowers are
      fragrant and the moon moves

with shadows. The balcony
   is noisy with piping and
      singing which is crisp and

sharp, and the swing in
   the courtyard is bathed in
      deep silence of the night.

默喚

林明理

在那鐘塔上
下望蜿蜒的河床,
小船兒點點
如碎銀一般!
彷彿從古老的風口裡
吹來一個浪漫的笛音,
穿越時空
驚起我心靈盤旋的
迴響。
我怎會忘記?
妳那凝思的臉,
伴隨這風中的淡香……
妳是我千年的期盼。
啊,布魯日,
小河裝著悠悠蕩漾的情傷,
而我,孤獨的,徘徊堤岸,
彷彿是中世紀才有著向晚!

Silent Calling

Lin Ming-Li

From the clock tower,
To look at the meandering river bed,
A speck after another speck of boat
To silver the boat like scattered coins!
As if from the ancient wind
Wafting here is a romantic fluting melody,
Through time and space
Stirring an echo in
My soul.
How can I forget?
Your face lost in a trance
With a faint fragrance in the wind....
You are my hope through a thousand years.
Oh, Bruges,
The small river contains overbrimming sorrow,
And I, solitarily, wander along the bank
Seemingly the dusk of Middle Ages only!

45.

海棠

蘇軾

東風嫋嫋泛崇光，香霧空濛月轉廊。
只恐夜深花睡去，故燒高燭照紅妝。

Chinese Crabapple Flowers   Su Shi

The east wind gently blows
   in spring, as fair as crabapple
      flowers. Flowery fragrance
in the fog, the moon is slowly
   moving past the corridor.
      Lest the flowers fall asleep

deep into the night, I hold
   a candle to admire them.

在愉悅夏夜的深邃處   林明理

從未忘記。
風雨摧蝕的
　　山海灣，
迎接耳語的浪花，
我們並肩跑往
　　遼闊的星野。

背後的風
古老漁村的想像——
　　恰如一個夢，
這路徑，錯落的腳印
　　和笑聲。

而今
在記憶中逐漸抹去的，
　　不是你逐浪的身影，
而是小小的思愁
　　隨波成藍色……
忽遠，又靠近了。

宋詩明理接千載
古今抒情詩三百首
漢英對照

In the Depth of a Pleasant Summer Night
Lin Ming-Li

Never forget.
The weather-beaten
    Mountain bay,
The waves whispering into ears,
Side by side we run
    To the boundless starry field.

The wind from the back
Imagination of an ancient fishing village —
    Like a dream,
The path, the random footprints
    And laughter.

Now
What gradually fades away from memory,
    Not your form chasing waves,
But a little longing
    To be blue with the waves ....
Suddenly afar, and is near again.

46·

惠崇《春江曉景》   蘇軾

竹外桃花三兩枝，春江水暖鴨先知。
蔞蒿滿地蘆芽短，正是河豚欲上時。

A Spring Scene by the River   Su Shi

Beyond the bamboo two or three
   fair twigs of peach flowers flare;
     the ducks are the first to feel

the warmth of water and spring.
   The ground is alive with worm-
     wood herbs and reed buds: it is

time for globefish to swim back
   into the river from the sea.

三月的微風   林明理

我在小石山邊徘徊,
柿子樹攀著孤帆,
河溪雀躍向前如一簇綠光的蝴蝶。
我把一切輕浮拋入長空,
冬天的莎車[15]歎息著
而晚鐘頻問三月雪。

The Gentle Wind of March   Lin Ming-Li

I loiter by a small rocky hill,
The persimmon tree lingers against a lonely sail,
The creek babbles forward like a green shaft of light as butterflies.
I cast all the frivolous things into the boundless sky,
Shache of Xinjiang Province is sighing in winter,
When the evening bell is beckoning the snow of March.

---

[15] 莎車位今新疆維吾爾自治區塔里木盆地西緣。

47·

花影 　　　　　　　　　　　　　　蘇軾

重重疊疊上瑤台,幾度呼童掃不開。
剛被太陽收拾去,卻教明月送將來。

Flowery Shadows 　　　　　　　Su Shi

Flowery shadows upon
　flowery shadows on the
　　pavilion; for several times
I ask the boy to sweep
　them away, all in vain.
　　The moment they are

collected by the fading
　sun, the bright moon
　　brings them back again.

月河把我帶進夢鄉 　　　　　　　林明理

　　　　獻給浮光躍金的北麗橋畔
　　　　　　　　　　　　——題記

一

夜風又把我帶進了
沿著月河畔的府城天堂——
那兒曾有舳艫相繼的文人墨客,
是黛樹如畫的水鄉。

在那迂迴的街巷外，
在那沉思的老城旁，
風把每首曲觴剪成了細雨，
輕拂我的臉，繾綣著牽掛。

而我是隻愛唱歌的灰雀，
從海峽飛向彼岸水驛，飛向
茶房和站船，臨橋的兜街
也走進了我的夢鄉。

二

五月的古樓月色如水，
多少個春秋已逝，
而你——鬢角也出現了銀色的光輝，
唯堅貞愛情的傳說，亙古不變。

正像舊民居演譯了所有舊時事，
讓歷史得以久長……
讓我也能夠向你獻上寄語，
以便記起重逢的淚水與歡喜的滋味。

啊，月河，你是江南水鄉的驕傲。
當我靜靜地誦讀你的時候，
就聽見你的回聲響在運河上，
恰似福爾摩沙睡眠中的夢幻。

宋詩明理逢千載
古今抒情詩三百首
漢英對照

The Moon River Brings Me Into My Dreamland
Lin Ming-Li

Dedicated to the Beili Bridge Brilliant with Gold and Light
— Preface

1.
Again the night wind brings me into
The paradise of Fucheng along the Moon River —
There have once been scholars & poets taking boats one after another,
A picturesque water town with dark trees.

Outside the winding streets,
Beside the contemplative old city,
The wind cuts each song into fine rain,
To brush my face, solicitous and lingering.

And I am a gray sparrow who loves to sing,
To fly from the straits to the water station on the other shore, to fly
To the teahouse and the boat station; the streets along the bridge
Also enter my dreamland.

2.
The moonlight over the ancient building in May is like water;
How many years have passed.
And you — your temples are with gray hairs.
Only the legend of faithful love remains unchanged.

Just as the old houses have interpreted all the past events,
For history to last forever....
Let me send you a message,
So as to remember the tears and joys of reunion.

Ah, the Moon River, you are the pride of the water town to the Southern Shore.
When I quietly read and recite you,
I hear your echo sounding over the canal,
Like the dream in Formosa's sleep.

---

48 ·

東欄梨花———和孔密州五絕之一 蘇軾

梨花淡白柳深青，柳絮飛時花滿城。
惆悵東欄一株雪，人生看得幾清明？

Pear Blossoms in My Courtyard Su Shi

Pear blossoms are delicately
   white when willow twigs are deeply
     green; willow catkins are fanning,

whirling, drifting, and wafting —
   filling the whole town. My heart,
     melancholy, is like the snow-

white pear blossoms against the
   eastern balustrade in my courtyard,
     and my limpid mind is detached

from the secular world of flashiness,
   noisiness, and transitoriness.

所謂永恆　　　　　　　　　　　　林明理

一枝綠柳銜來一個春天，
把難以揣測的大地吻醒，
讓理念在一剎那間
倏閃，相思成雪。

The So-called Eternity　　　Lin Ming-Li

A twig of green willow brings a spring,
To kiss and awaken the unfathomable earth,
For the idea in an instant
To flash, lovesickness into snow.

49·

琴詩　　　　　　　　　　　　　蘇軾

若言琴上有琴聲，放在匣中何不鳴？
若言聲在指頭上，何不於君指上聽？

On the Chinese Lute　　　　Su Shi

If we say music is produced
　　from the Chinse lute itself, why,
　　　　when it is put back into the box,

there is no more voice? If we say
　　musical notes are coaxed from
　　　　between the fingers of the player,

why, with wonder, cannot we
    play a tune just with our fingers?

平靜的湖面   林明理

在淡淡白色煙霧裡
你是思索中的詩人
看落葉褪盡
季節輪換的容貌

The Calm Lake   Lin Ming-Li

In the thin white fog
You are a poet lost in deep thought
At the sight of leaves all shedding
The changing visage of a new season

縱筆三首（其一）   蘇軾

寂寂東坡一病翁，白鬚蕭散滿霜風。
小兒誤喜朱顏在，一笑那知是酒紅。

Three Random Pieces (1)   Su Shi

Old now, good days no more, I'm
    down and helpless with various
        diseases and ailments; I'm silver-

宋詩明理接千載
古今抒情詩三百首
漢英對照

streaked, long and loose, like the life-
    long frosty wind which never abates.
        Seeing my flushed face, my little son

mistakes it for a sign of youth —
    the truth comes out through my laughter
        in spite of myself: red from liquor.

當你變老   林明理

不管你信不信
我篤定
當你變老
我仍會看著月光
傳遞祝福及
    索取一個吻
是的，我們的相知
是非比尋常的——
我常想起曾經讀過的詩
並珍藏在黝藍的星空
它讓我歡笑
    也讓我憂愁
而你就是原因

When You Are Old   Lin Ming-Li

You believe it or not
I am sure
When you are old
I will still look at the moon
To pass on blessings and
    To ask for a kiss
Yes, our acquaintance
Is quite unusual —

I often think of the poems I have read
To treasure them up in the dark blue sky
It makes me laugh
    It also makes me worry
And you are the cause

51·

題臨安邸   林升

山外青山樓外樓，西湖歌舞幾時休？
暖風熏得遊人醉，直把杭州作汴州。

Written in an Inn of the New Capital
Lin Sheng

Hills beyond blue hills, mansions
   upon mansions; in the warm wind
     there is a faint vibration of occasional

noises of trumpeting, twanging, strumming,
   singing, dancing, and snatches of laughter,
     resounding through the West Lake —

when to rest? In such a charming air,
   the travelers are fairly heady and drunken
     with all this exhilaration; an immoderate

share of the pleasures of Hangzhou deprives
   them of the fond memory of their old capital.

黃昏,賽納河[16]

林明理

你當記得,那天空
憂傷而美麗,波光與船燈互耀
而我癡迷於美的憧憬
癡迷於岸邊的街頭熱舞
周邊玫瑰色的迷濛
那艾菲爾鐵塔,我所愛的王者
在充滿愛情的手中入睡
金色光座如聖體晃耀
一座座拱橋穿越夜的虛無
靜靜地養神中
在光影交織的大氣裡
噢,賽納河,我愛
你的閃光在我們之間交織
就像惜別時星辰的回眸

Dusk, Seine River[17]

Lin Ming-Li

You shall remember, the sky
Sorrowful and splendid, light from waves and lamps from boats mutually shine
I am obsessed with the vision of beauty
With hot street dance by the shore
Rosy mistiness in the neighborhood
The Eiffel Tower, the king I love
Asleep in the hands brimful of love

---

[16] 塞納河(Seine)是流經巴黎市中心的法國第二大河,許多重要建築都圍繞著塞納河兩岸,它也是巴黎的母親河。

[17] The Seine is the second largest river in France which flows through the center of Paris, its two banks boasting many important buildings, for which it is deemed as the mother of Paris.

The golden seat shimmers like a host
One after another arch bridge goes through the emptiness of the night
In quiet repose
In the atmosphere intermingled with light and shadow
Oh, the Seine, I love
Your flash interweaves between us
Like the backward glance upon parting from the stars

52·

曉出淨慈寺送林子方　　　　　楊萬里

畢竟西湖六月中，風光不與四時同。
接天蓮葉無窮碧，映日荷花別樣紅。

The Charming West Lake　　　Yang Wanli

July reveals the beauty of the West
　Lake which is unique through the
　　four seasons: lotus leaves growing

endless, to green the boundless
　sky; lotus flowers, caught
　　in the sun, are charmingly red.

西湖，你的名字在我聲音裡　　　林明理

西湖，你的名字在我聲音裡
來得多麼可喜，轉得多麼光潔

就像秋月與星辰，不為逝去的陽光哭泣
只跟雨說話，為大地而歌
我在風中，呼喚你，像新月一樣
升到山巔同白晝擦肩而過
四周是鳥語與花香的喜悅
而你宛若夢境，湖光把我推向極遠處

西湖，你的名字在我聲音裡
來得多麼輕快，轉得多麼遼闊
就像飛鳥與狂雪，不為逝去的陽光哭泣
只跟風說話，為山谷而歌
我在風中，凝望你，像雲彩一樣
升到深邃的繁星世界，輕輕搖曳
開始唱歌，而你在夢境邊緣
——我是追逐白堤岸柳的風

West Lake, Your Name Is in My Voice

Lin Ming-Li

West Lake, your name is in my voice
How gratifying it is, how bright it turns
Like the autumn moon and stars, no weeping for the spent sunshine
Just talk with the rain, sing for the great earth
In the wind, I am calling you, like a new moon
Rising atop the mountain to brush against the day
All about it is the joy of birdsongs and flowery scent
You are like a dream, and the lake light pushes me afar

West Lake, your name is in my voice
How swiftly it comes, how vast it turns
Like flying birds and wild snow, no weeping for the spent sunshine

Just talk to the wind, sing for the valley
In the wind, I am gazing at you, like a blossom of cloud
Rising to the profound starry world, swaying gently
Starting to sing, and you are on the edge of a dream
— I am the wind chasing the willows along the white embankment

53．

小池 　　　　　　　　　　　　　　　楊萬里

泉眼無聲惜細流，樹陰照水愛晴柔。
小荷才露尖尖角，早有蜻蜓立上頭。

A Small Pond 　　　　　　　　　Yang Wanli

Trickling streams of water are
　　silently and cautiously escaping
　　　　from the eye of the fountain;

the reflected shadows of trees
　　on water love zephyr in days fine.
　　　　A tender lotus leaf is cutting a fine

figure above water, when a playful
　　dragonfly flies to settle on it.

靜靜的湖 　　　　　　　　　　　　林明理

靜靜的湖，
如拉斐爾手繪的聖母。

人在畫中走，
綠是一種顏色。
在粧點華美的小舟上。
我凝神看了又看，
啊，就這樣──
放慢了腳步，依偎著繆斯笑了。

The Quiet Lake   Lin Ming-Li

The quiet lake,
Like the Virgin Mary hand-painted by Raphael.
People walk in the painting,
Green is a color.
On the beautifully decorated boat.
I gaze and stare at it,
Ah, thus it is —
I slow down my steps, smiling against Muse.

54·

閒居初夏午睡起二絕句（其一）　　楊萬里

梅子留酸軟齒牙，芭蕉分綠與窗紗。
日長睡起無情思，閑看兒童捉柳花。

Waking Up From an Early Summer Nap (No. 1 of 2 poems)   Yang Wanli

In early summer, the sight
　of plums is suggestive of
　　a sour taste which softens

my teeth; the plantain tree
　　waves its leaves against the
　　　　window, sharing its greenness.

A lengthy day sees me napping
　　and waking up, my mind still
　　　　blunt and slow and, through

listless hours, I languidly watch
　　the children running and catching
　　　　at willow catkins, an idle play.

初夏　　　　　　　　　　　　　　林明理

1.
北極光
從大冰原島流出。
甦醒的萬物不變,
唯岩脊的花,嘎吱嘆息。

2.
古老森林
是人類最後一塊寶土

3.
蜂鳥飛行如細雨,
迎接初夏的耳語,
展開交配季。

4.
飛鼠初來乍到,
滑翔......
到伊甸園的樹洞。

5.
鯡魚群
像細密閃亮的星宿
歡快洄遊。

6.
一隻灰鯨
跋涉萬里
發出牠的歌聲。

7.
母熊帶著孩子
像漫畫故事裡的
女戰士。

8.
這最後一片荒野，
是地球最後的秘密。

9.
唯一沉默的
是整片莎草地。

10.
而我站在這裡，
與我的上主說話，
如通往伊甸園的
那條路。

The Early Summer   Lin Ming-Li

1.
Northern lights
Flow out of the Great Ice Island.
Myriads of things that wake up seem to be unchanged,
Only the flowers atop rock ridge are crunching and sighing.

2.
The ancient forest
Is the last treasure land of mankind

3.
Hummingbirds fly like a drizzle,
To greet the whispers of the early summer,
Thus to begin the season of mating.

4.
The flying squirrel has just arrived,
Gliding....
To the tree hole in the Garden of Eden.

5.
A school of herring
Like a maze of splendid small stars
Joyful migration.

6.
A gray whale
Travels ten thousand kilometers
While singing all the way.

7.
A female bear with her baby
Like the female warrior
In a comic book.

8.
This last wilderness
Is the last secret of the earth.
9.
The only spot that is silent
Is the vast field of sedge.

10.
And I am standing here,
Talking to my Lord,
Like the road leading
To the Garden of Eden.

55 ·

小雨   楊萬里

雨來細細複疏疏，縱不能多不肯無。
似妒詩人山入眼，千峰故隔一簾珠。

A Slight Rain   Yang Wanli

A slight rain is sprinkling, spraying,
    drizzling, drozzling, like fine incessant
        needles of water which are playing

in the air, before drifting down, instead
 of tapering off. Jealous of the poet's
  eyeful of green mountains which

are dim and distant? A curtain of
 beads of rain is made, to screen off
  peaks upon peaks, ineffectually.

秋雨，總是靜靜地下著……　　　　林明理

十月最後的一抹暮色
一切都是那麼寧靜
一隻黑鳥悄悄靠近
　　悄悄離開
哦　朋友
　　……我沒有忘記
　　又怎能忘記……
我似鼓翼的蛾
　　努力向前
　　　永不墜落
也許，你也在夜雨中
　　等待雲霧散開
讓我想像
　　在遙遠的過去
我們曾經一起
　　走入光芒裡
你的輕言細語
讓我滿耳充滿幸福

Autumn Rain Always Falls Quietly……

Lin Ming-Li

The last twilight of October
Everything is so quiet
A blackbird approaches quietly
    And leaves quietly
Oh   my friend
    ….I have not forgotten
    How can I forget….
Like a fluttering moth
    I strive forward
        Never to drop
Perhaps, you are also in the night rain
    Waiting for the clouds to disperse
For me to imagine
    In the distant past
We have ever walked
    together into the light
Your soft and tender words
Fill my ears with happiness

56·

池州翠微亭

岳飛

經年塵土滿征衣，特特尋芳上翠微。
好水好山看不足，馬蹄催趁月明歸。

The Green Pavilion   Yue Fei

Year in year out my army
　uniform is soiled with dust;
　　now idle, I come to the Green

Pavilion on horseback in
　search of flowery scent.
　　Before my eyes are feasted

with fair hills and fair rills,
　the clip-clop brings me home-
　　ward in bright moonlight.

倒影   林明理

我曾夢想
為你搭起一座心房
那兒星光璀璨，林邊
到處飛舞著歌雀的翅膀

而我
是日日夜夜拂過的輕風
從繁花似錦的草原落到
你沉思默想的河畔

在我無數的回眸中
不管我立在東方或西岸
都將聽見一種曲調
那是水波激蕩著你唱吟的地方

Reflection

Lin Ming-Li

I have ever dreamed
Of building house of a heart for you
Where the stars shine brightly, the edge of the woods
Is alive with the fluttering wings of songbirds

And I am
The breeze which blows away day and night
From the grassland filled with flowers
To the riverside by which you meditate

In my countless backward glances
Whether I stand in the east or on the west bank
Audible is the same melody
The place where the waves stir your into singing

---

57 ·

約客

趙師秀

黃梅時節家家雨，青草池塘處處蛙。
有約不來過夜半，閑敲棋子落燈花。

Waiting in Simple Idleness for My Playmate

Zhao Shixiu

In a steadily streaming summer rain
all roofs are caught, when grassy ponds,
big and small, far and near, are alive

with croaking frogs. Midnight finds
me waiting for my playmate, and
beating the table, in simple idleness,

with a chessman, hard enough to make
it vibrate slightly, the lamp flickering
through the solitude of the night.

冥想 林明理

多思慕你
邊馳騁,邊微笑
像飛魚在水花間躍動
這是因為有普羅旺斯
夏日才這般夢幻
還是山丘上那片愛情花海
讓我斜倚著,向宇宙說話

Meditation Lin Ming-Li

How I envy you
Galloping and smiling
Like flying fish flashing in the splashing water
It is because of Provence
Summer is so dreamy
Still the field of flowers of love on the hill
Against which I lean, while talking to the universe

宋詩明理搓千載
古今抒情詩三百首
漢英對照

58．

春日偶成　　　　　　　　　　　　　程顥

雲淡風輕近午天，傍花隨柳過前川。
時人不識餘心樂，將謂偷閒學少年。

An Impromptu Poem on a Spring Day
Cheng Hao

Pale clouds and a light breeze
   approach the noon; under willows
     and beside flowers I stroll along

the river bank. Worldly people
   know not the joy of my heart,
     which remains as lucid as a mirror

— they say I snatch a little
   leisure from the rush of business,
     acting like a naughty boy.

雲淡，風清了　　　　　　　　　　林明理

把愛琴海上諸神泥塑成圓頂的鐘塔
回歸
寧靜

你看，那夕陽下的風車
天真地在海邊唱遊
那碧波的點點白帆
輕撫著客中的寂寞

啜著咖啡;青天
自淺紅
至深翠
沖淡濃潤的綠,白色的牆
耳際只有草底的鳴蟲
抑抑悲歌……

The Clouds Are Pale and the Winds Are Crisp
　　　　　　　　　　　　Lin Ming-Li

A bell tower with a dome made of clay from the Aegean gods
To return
To tranquility

Look, the windmill under the sunset
Is singing innocently by the sea
Dots after dots of white sails against the blue waves
Are caressing the loneliness among guests

Sipping coffee; the blue sky
From light red
To deep green
Diluting the rich green, white walls
My ears are ringing with the chirping of insects in the grass
A sorrowful song……

59 ·

秋月   程顥

清溪流過碧山頭，空水澄鮮一色秋。
隔斷紅塵三十裡，白雲紅葉兩悠悠。

The Autumn Moon   Cheng Hao

A clear river runs past the
   green hill; the limpid water
      and the blue sky constitute

a scroll of autumnal painting.
   The mortal world has been
      isolated thirty miles away:

white clouds in the sky float
   freely and red leaves in
      the hill spread leisurely.

秋之楓   林明理

入夜
深谷裡
一棵棵楓忍住呻吟
那伸長的手臂
像雨中飛燕
拍搏著眼中長出的愁緒

The Maples of Autumn   Lin Ming-Li

The night advances
In the deep valley

One after another maple refrains from moaning
The outstretched arms
Like swallows in the rain
Are struggling against the sorrow from their eyes

60.

題淮南寺　　　　　　　　　　　程顥

南去北來休便休，白蘋吹盡楚江秋。
道人不是悲秋客，一任晚山相對愁。

Inscription on Huinan Temple
Cheng Hao

From the north to the south,
　as free as the air. The autumn
　　wind blows white duckweed

traceless on the Southern River.
　A Zen master is no sentimentalist
　　of the desolate autumn scene,

in spite of the mutual sorrow
　of opposite hills at eventide.

樹林入口　　　　　　　　　　　林明理

時間是水塘交替的光影
它的沉默浸滿了我的瞳仁

雨沖出凹陷的泥地
在承接暗藍的蒼穹
一隻小彎嘴畫眉
正叼走最後一顆晨星

呵四季從不懂謊言
就像我的心啊
披滿十一月秋天
除了想你已無處躲藏
當太陽掠過樺樹上端
索性把思念變成一條小溪
讓重疊的濃綠時時潺潺鳴響

Entrance to the Woods Lin Ming-Li

Time is the alternating light & shadow over the pond
Its silence fills my pupils
Rain breaks out of the sunken mud
To accept the dark-blue sky
A small curve-mouthed thrush
Is taking away the last morning star

Oh, the four seasons never know lies
Oh like my heart
Covered with the autumn of November
Nowhere to hide except for missing you
When the sun rises over the top of birch trees
Simply to turn your thoughts into a stream
For the overlapping green to gurgle from time to time

61．

江上漁者　　　　　　　　　　　范仲淹

江上往來人，但愛鱸魚美。
君看一葉舟，出沒風波裡。

A Riverside Fisherman　　　Fan Zhongyan

All river-side fishermen
   love delicious perch, and
      they are busy fishing. Lo,

a fisherman on a leaf of boat:
   appearing and disappearing,
      in and out of perilous waves.

渡口　　　　　　　　　　　　林明理

翩翩的灰面鷲，
穿越了烏溪的落日，
要飛進星海的岸浪了。

岸浪是冰天一片哪，
俯瞰而下，只有遠山守候，
又有什麼可以長久？

槳聲驚動的水鳥嗎？
八卦平台的遊客嗎？
亦或不受羈絆的霜風？

在天地相接的盡頭，
漁火隱隱，

你聽，故鄉的小溪又唱了，
誰說，萬物皆易老，
更看空濛的水月中？

今夜，街燈淡蕩，
岸上的舟子已歇，
而我憶往的夢顯現了，
剎時，亭上的鈴音又獨自飄響了。

The Ferry   Lin Ming-Li

The flying grey-faced buzzard
Has crossed the sunset of the Black Creek,
And is to fly into the waves to the shore of the starry sea.

The bankside waves are great sheet of icy sky,
Overlooking, only distant mountains keep waiting,
Then what can last for ever?
The water birds started by the paddling oar?
The visitors to the Eight Diagrams Platform?
Or the frosty wind free of any restraint?

At the end where the sky meets the earth,
The fisherman's fire is dimly discernible,
Listen, the native brook is singing again,
Who says that everything ages easily,
And to look into the misty moon in the water?

Tonight, the street lights are dimly flickering,
The boats ashore are at rest,
And my dream of the past appears;
All of a sudden, the solitary bell on the pavilion is ringing again.

62．

出守桐廬道中   范仲淹

素心愛雲水，此日東南行。
笑解塵纓處，滄浪無限情。

An Outing   Fan Zhongyan

By nature I like roaming
  as flowing clouds and running
    water; and now I get a chance

to make a southeastward journey.
  Coming to the side of the Rich
    Spring River, I laugh heartily,

taking off my tasseled hat soiled
  from dust, my heart gladdens with
    joyful emotion which is boundless.

春草   林明理

小舟
一如萍藻遊魚
把明窗外的
小橋、亭台
新禾、梯田
都一同蕩漾
在一隻踽步的鷺鷥中
漸遠漸細的是富春江畔

輕風拂過，淺紅淡青
那粉牆黛瓦
隱於畔旁老樹一株
偶來砧杵聲
穿越山林
打起了呆然的回應
該如何想像如何放散而又彌望
竹花枝梗正在凝碧
而我已聽見了　流泉　浪翻

Spring Grass

Lin Ming-Li

A small boat
Like a fish swimming through the lake of duckweeds
Without the window
Small bridges, kiosks
New seedlings, terraces
All are rippling together
In the roaming of a pair of egrets
What tapers off is the bank of Fuchun River

Gentle wind blowing, pink and light green
The red wall and the black tiles
Hidden by an old bankside tree
Occasionally the sound of beating clothes
Travels through the mountain forest
Echoing woodenly
How to imagine and scatter and gaze afar
Bamboo twigs and leaves are gathering green
And I have heard the running fountain and churning waves

63 •

蠶婦　　　　　　　　　　　　　張俞

昨日入城市，歸來淚滿巾。
遍身羅綺者，不是養蠶人。

A Silk-woman　　　　　　　Zhang Yu

A silk-woman enters the city
　　to sell her cocoon fiber, and she
　　　　returns with a kerchief soaked

with tears: among the crowds
　　of silk wearers there, she fails
　　　　to find a single silkworm raiser.

江岸暮色　　　　　　　　　　林明理

滿枝杏葉的樹叢
像是空山的彩蝶
緩緩飛來
靜聽
松濤
在依依的薄染
層巒疊翠的雲霞
更有幾點歸雁
悲鳴
滿霜風
月寒前
夕陽
送潮在
天之一角與隔岸的傳鐘

The River Shore Veiled in Dusk

Lin Ming-Li

The apricot trees green with foliage
Like the colorful butterflies in the empty mountain
Flying slowly
To listen quietly
To the waves of pine trees
In the lingering color
Layers upon layers of clouds
A few dots of wild geese return
Sorrowful wailing
The wind full of frost
Before it is cold
The setting sun
Is moving tides
The ringing bell from the other shore and the corner of the world

---

64 ·

陶者

梅堯臣

陶盡門前土，屋上無片瓦。
十指不沾泥，鱗鱗居大廈。

The Potter-worker

Mei Yaochen

The earth in front of his door
　has been dug to be used up,
　　but his own house is still a

thatched one. Those whose
   fingers are not soiled, live
      in grand tiled mansions.

山間小路   　　　　　　　　　　　林明理

深入山丘的陰影
細細領略
臘梅的清香

遠樹凝寂
從寺塔鐘樓走出
在墨潑間
在花雨上

想心定的水塘
被日落的叢林圍繞
從許多蜿蜒的小路
遠離霧氣的瀰漫在村莊

A Path in the Mountain   　　Lin Ming-Li

Into the shadow of mountain
To sense carefully
The faint scent of wintersweet

Still are the remote trees
Out of the bell tower of the temple
The instant of ink spreading
On the flowery rain

The pool is ready to calm down
And is surrounded by the woods caught in the setting sun
From a lot of meandering paths
Away from the village veiled in mist

65 ·

寒菊 　　　　　　　　　　　　　　　　　鄭思肖

花開不並百花叢，獨立疏籬趣未窮。
寧可枝頭抱香死，何曾吹落北風中。

Cold Chrysanthemums 　　　　　Zheng Sixiao

bloom in autumn when a hundred
　　flowers fade; by hedge-side your
　　solitary sentiment is boundless.

Even if dead, you cling to stems
　　and twigs, instead of reconciling
　　yourself to the north wind.

在瀟瀟的雪夜 　　　　　　　　　　　　林明理

我走過一條黯淡的野道，
正月裡湖波返射的雪林
使晚天那初升的月空寂，輕漾。
一聲兩聲罄鈸在每一個角落
像崖壁斷下的故風細雨，
輕輕地飄飛、隱沒。
突然，枝上三兩烏鴉
無情無緒地叫著，
從前方泥濘的黑路
飛入樹底盡頭。

也許在無數的失落中
那藏在忍冬蔦蘿的葉堆裡，
傳來微弱的某種聲音，
似乎告訴我，
它知道　生何其短促！
而我發現，昨日的枯樹
竟長出新綠時，笑了。

A Snowy Night Noisy with Wind
Lin Ming-Li

I walk along a dark road in the wilderness,
In January the snowy forest reflecting waves of the lake,
And the initial moon in the night sky is lonesome, rippling.
One or two cymbal sounds echoing in each corner,
Like the old wind and fine rain beneath the cliff,
Gently floating, disappearing.
Suddenly, three or two crows on the branch
Are cawing numbly,
From the dark, muddy road ahead
To fly to the bottom of the trees.
Perhaps from countless losses
From the hidden piles of honeysuckle leaves,
Travels a weak voice,
Which seems to tell me:
It knows　how brief life is!
And I find that yesterday's withered trees
Are eventually bursting with new green, and I am all smiles.

66·

梅　　　　　　　　　　　　　　　　　　　王淇

不受塵埃半點侵，竹籬茅舍自甘心。
只因誤識林和靖，惹得詩人說到今。

The Plum Flower　　　　　　　　　Wang Qi

is not soiled by mortal dust,
　and it reconciles itself to
　　the company of bamboo

hedges and thatched cottages.
　When someday it is married
　　to Lin Hejing, a poet-lover

of the plum flower, praises
　shower on it until today.

禪月　　　　　　　　　　　　　　　　　林明理

正如三月櫻
當粉紅與湛藍
落在
金池裡
你可以忘卻
那春天關在窗外
被一枝雪捕住的瞬間，

當若水的心境
擴成林濤之月
如天宇間的

一粒征塵
要在輕醉中搏擊歷史的岸邊。

The Moon of Zen   Lin Ming-Li

Like the cherry of March
When pink and deep blue
Fall
In the golden pond
You can forget
The instant when spring is shut without the window
And is caught by a branchful of snow

When the frame of mind is like water
Expanding into the moon of forest waves
Like a mote of dust
Between heaven and earth
Throbbing against the bank of history when slightly drunken

湖上   徐元傑

花開紅樹亂鶯啼，草長平湖白鷺飛。
風日晴和人意好，夕陽簫鼓幾船歸。

On the West Lake   Xu Yuanjie

In the trees red with a riotous
    profusion of red flowers, a
        bevy of orioles are twittering

宋詩明理接千載
古今抒情詩三百首
漢英對照

    and frolicking; the lakeside grass
       is lush and bevies of white
          egrets are flying and wheeling

over the calm lake. The east
   wind blows warm in a fine day,
      people enjoying a happy frame

of mind; in the setting sun, a few
   painted boats, noisy with piping
      music, are slowly heading home.

光之湖   林明理

春日帶著白松味
罩在橡樹叢
石岸旁
雨露殘留未散
我在虛空裡逡巡——
那失足的花葉
還有從歌雀銜來的漿果
闖入了自己眼眸
常春藤恆長著
蟲聲起了騷動
一隻赤松鼠忽地躍起
轆轆的馬車呼嘯而過

The Lake of Light   Lin Ming-Li

Spring is redolent of white pine
Veiled in oak trees
By the rocky bank
Dew remains

I wander in the void —
The stray flowers and leaves
And berries from song-sparrows
Invade his own eyes
Ivy is on the growing
Insects on the chirping
A red squirrel suddenly leaps up
The rumbling carriage is flying away

68 •

村晚　　　　　　　　　　　　　　雷震

草滿池塘水滿陂，山銜落日浸寒漪。
牧童歸去橫牛背，短笛無腔信口吹。

A Village at Eventide　　　　　Lei Zhen

A grassy pond is filled with water
　to its brim; the mountain holds a
　　setting sun in its mouth to be dipped

in cold water. A herd-boy sits astride
　on ox back, toying with a small flute
　　which produces random music.

霧　　　　　　　　　　　　　　林明理

在故鄉紅石崗的坡上
牽出了
我家老山羊匿在銀月裡玩

夢見了
那是辣子，或是包穀
門檻還有許多菜香

阿公揹我
為我淌汗
而我滿心歡喜
因為金星星繡滿了我紅搖籃

Fog   Lin Ming-Li

On the native slope of red rocky hillock
I get out
The old goat in my family to be hidden for play in the silver moon

In my dream
I see capsicum, or corn
The doorsill fragrant with a lot of vegetables

My grandpa carries me on his back
To sweat for me
And my heart is filled with joys
Since the golden stars are embroidered with my red cradles

69·

清明   王禹偁

無花無酒過清明，興味蕭然似野僧。
昨日鄰家乞新火，曉窗分與讀書燈。

Pure Brightness Day   Wang Yucheng

Without flowers and without
   wine I while away the Pure
      Brightness Day, without interest

and without taste, I'm like
   a restless and helpless old
      monk. Yesterday I get my

kitchen fire from my neighbor
   after the fireless day, and the
      dawn finds my window bright

with a lamp, and it beams at my
   pleasure of nightlong reading.

在我的眼睛深處   林明理

我站在環繞岩頂的天空下，
對每個自然的元素
充滿著生命之外的召喚，
它來自玫瑰雲朵的後方。
一棵扭曲的橡樹
伸向廣闊天邊；
烏鴉在翱翔中揮去憂鬱的意志。
這墳丘，面對被太陽鍍金的海上，
暗暗地笑談亙古的憶往。
一切歷史悲劇
全都碎裂於大浪。
在它平靜地接受——

緩緩的逝去前，
如何能預料未來所揭示的理想？
那天使透明的翅膀
從黝黑的世界
飛向深邃的蔚藍，
我看見你在我的眼睛深處
優越地　閃光……

In the Depth of My Eyes　　　　Lin Ming-Li

I stand under the sky with rocky peaks,
Each natural element
Is charged with the calling from beyond life;
It comes from the rear of rosy clouds.
A twisted oak tree
Stretches out to the boundless horizon;
In their flight, the crows whip away gloomy moods.
The grave, facing the sea gilded by the sun,
Is secretly talking laughingly about the old memories.
All historical tragedies
Are smashed to pieces in the breakers.
Calmly it accepts —
Before slow disappearance,
How to expect the ideal revealed in the future?
The angels' transparent wings
From the dark world
Fly to the deep blue;
I see, in the depth of my eyes
You are proudly glittering……

70 ·

初夏遊張園　　　　　　　　　　　　　戴敏

乳鴨池塘水淺深，熟梅天氣半晴陰。
東園載酒西園醉，摘盡枇杷一樹金。

Visiting Parks in Early Summer　　Dai Min

Ducklings are frolicking in
　the pond with water deep or
　　shallow; plums are ripe when

it is half cloudy and half fine.
　We buy wine in the east park
　　to drink ourselves drunk in

the west park; the trees are
　golden with loquats which
　　are picked as we please.

夏荷　　　　　　　　　　　　　　　　林明理

帶著一種堅強的溫柔
從西湖中凝望
這個風月無邊的
琉璃世界

是翠鳥兒？還是岸柳拂袖
遊魚也永不疲乏的
簇擁向我

那亭台之月，悄悄披上煙霧

來看流水
就是看不盡
一絲凜然的
荷影
夜的帷幕裡的光點

Summer Lotus   Lin Ming-Li

With a firm gentleness
Gazing from the West Lake
At the glass world
With boundless view

Is it a kingfisher? Or the bankside willows tugging at sleeves?
The tirelessly swimming fish
Are clustering about me

The moon above the pavilion, stealthily misted
To see the running water
Inexhaustible is the sight
A shade of graceful
Lotus shadows
Dots of light from the curtain of night

71·

七夕   楊樸

未會牽牛意若何，須邀織女織金梭。
年年乞與人間巧，不道人間巧已多。

Double Seventh Eve   Yang Pu

What is the mindset of the Herd-
   boy? Why should he invite the
      Weaver-girl, to weave together

with a golden shuttle a skyful
   of rosy clouds? From year to year
      cleverness and dexterity are

begged from on high, not knowing
   that cleverness and dexterity
      abound in the mortal world.

秋夕   林明理

在地球、月亮和海水的無垠中
我用愛與友誼的目光凝視著。我喜歡沿她
奧妙的燦亮走，使我感到很渺小，很迷失
我將牽繫於窗外她輝耀之所在
並感覺其神秘的沉寂注視著我的悲愁
至於那古老的傳說，早已通過無數個世紀
當然，往往是美麗而恆久的。

Autumn Eve   Lin Ming-Li

In the boundlessness of the earth,
the moon and the sea,
I gaze with the eyes of love and friendship.
I'd like to walk along her
Wonderful lamp makes me feel small and lost.
I will be tied to the place
where she shines outside the window

And feel her mysterious silence
watching my sorrow.
As for the age-old legend,
through countless centuries,
Of course, it still is beautiful and eternal.

72.

夜坐 　　　　　　　　　　　　　　　　張耒

庭戶無人秋月明，夜霜欲落氣先清。
梧桐真不甘衰謝，數葉迎風尚有聲。

A Night View 　　　　　　　　　　　Zhang Lei

Soulless and voiceless, the court-
　yard is bathed in the flood of autumn
　　moon; on the verge of hoar frost

descending, the air is clear and crisp.
　The parasol tree is standing straight
　　in the yard, not reconciling itself

to the fading and falling of leaves,
　a few of which are still dancing
　　and prattling in the wind all round.

雨夜 　　　　　　　　　　　　　　　　林明理

夜路中，沒有
一點人聲也沒有燈影相隨。

在山樹底盡頭,眼所觸
都是清冷,撐起
一把藍綠的小傘,等妳。

雨露出它長腳般的足跡,
細點兒地踩遍了
疊石結成的小徑,讓我在沙泥中
心似流水般地孤寂。

我用寒衫披上了我的焦慮,
幾片落葉的微音,卻聽到
那連接無盡的秋風細雨
竟在四野黯黑中出現和我一樣的心急……

The Rainy Night   Lin Ming-Li

Along the night road, without
Any human sound, without light and shadow.
Beyond the trees on the mountain, within sight
All is coldness, holding
A small green umbrella, waiting for you.

The rain reveals its long footsteps,
In tiny steps to trample
All the stony paths, for me in the sand
To be solitary with a heart like the running water.

With humble clothes I wear my worries,
The gentle voice of a few falling leaves, audible
The autumn wind and drizzle connecting endlessly
Should share the same worry with me with four walls of darkness……

73.

牧童詩 　　　　　　　　　　　　　　　　　　　黃庭堅

騎牛遠遠過前村，短笛橫吹隔隴聞。
多少長安名利客，機關用盡不如君。

The Herd-boy: a Gainer of Life
　　　　　　　　　　　　　　　　　　　Huang Tingjian

The herd-boy sits on an ox,
　　passing by a distant mountain
　　　　village, slowly and leisurely,

while producing random
　　tunes from his flute: audible
　　　　across the fields. In the capital

how many seekers of fame
　　and gains: seeking, searching,
　　　　and pursuing here and there,

high and low, eventually
　　are losers, instead of gainers.

稻草人 　　　　　　　　　　　　　　　　　　　林明理

在雲遮紅日的天穹
我輕旋窺看，
嘟嘟嚷嚷，於晨星隱退時
出現了你雙眼溫情的模樣
那是我的思想、我的蔚藍，我的海洋；

悄然的,是十里的露珠
屏住了呼吸
跟著我仔細端詳
告訴我,這可是天使的足音?
還是寂寞的薰染?……

我張開臂膀,雀躍奔跑,
卻傳來一陣清澈的聲響－
如一道道金霞,置身故鄉,
那一身叮咚的、褪色的布衣
早已披滿了與你邂逅的稻浪……

The Scarecrow　　　　　　　　Lin Ming-Li

In the sky where the red sun is hidden behind the clouds,
I spin gently to get a peep,
Mumbling, when morning stars fade,
A pair of your gentle eyes appear,
Which are my mind, my azure, my ocean;

Stealthily, dewdrops for ten miles
Hold their breath,
Following me to gaze carefully.
Tell me, are they the footsteps of angels?
Or scented loneliness?　……

I stretch my arms, running and scampering,
When a clear sound is traveling —
Like beams of golden glow, in native place,
The clinging faded cotton clothes
Are filled with rice waves which encounter you……

74 ·

上蕭家峽 　　　　　　　　　　　　　　　　黃庭堅

玉筍峰前幾百家，山明松雪水明沙。
趁虛人集春蔬好，桑菌竹萌煙蕨芽。

Going to Xiaojia Gorge 　　　　　Huang Tingjian

Beneath Yusi Mountain there
　are hundreds of households;
　　the mountain boasts bright

snow among pines and clear
　sand in the river bed. The market
　　day sees crowds of people and

plentiful spring vegetables:
　mushrooms and bamboo shoots
　　and fiddlehead ferns, and what not.

正月的融雪 　　　　　　　　　　　　　　　林明理

在最遙遠的北方，
那揚威的落影我窺視激越，
它們遮蔽彩虹和天梯的距離，
恰似吟泣的重圓。正月的融雪。

槐花相思不變，
羞紅間又披上山雨，
於是急急走尋的風
貼進張望：一株探頭的花兒，
一片葉，一顆星，
都紛紛投遞——再熟悉不過的笛音。

The Thawing Snow of the Second Moon
Lin Ming-Li

In the remotest north,
I peer at the majestic falling shadows with excitement,
They block the distance between the rainbow and the heavenly ladder,
Like the weeping reunion. The thawing snow of the second moon.
The love of locust flowers is constant,
The shy redness is veiled in a mountain rain,
And the wind in a great hurry
Comes close to look: a flower raising its stem,
A leaf, a star,
Gradually to send off — the most familiar fluting sound.

75 ·

睡起
黃庭堅

柿葉鋪庭紅顆秋，熏爐沉水度衣篝。
松風夢與故人遇，同駕飛鴻跨九州。

Awake from a Sleep
Huang Tingjian

Deep autumn: persimmon
　　leaves blanket the courtyard,
　　　　when the trees are bedecked

with red persimmons; the censer
　　is curling with smoke, and wisp
　　　　after wisp of scent is arising

from the bamboo clothes warmer.
　　A distant dream: in spells and spells
　　　　of pine wind, I meet my old friend

and, riding on a wild goose, we
　　tour nine states of the Divine Land.

貓尾花　　　　　　　　　　　　　　　　　林明理

此刻綠光的湖岸仍隱蔽，
白夜漸次化開；
無樹的草坡裡沒有任何騷動，
不久，紫色的貓尾花將跟太陽同步說話。

The Cattail Flower　　　　　　　Lin Ming-Li

Now the green lake shore is still concealed,
The white night gradually melts away;
No commotion in the treeless grassy slope,
Soon, the purple cattail flower will talk to the sun at the same time.

76·

夜發分寧寄杜澗叟　　　　　　　　　　　黃庭堅

陽關一曲水東流，燈火旌陽一釣舟。
我自只如常日醉，滿川風月替人愁。

Night Journey to Fenning   Huang Tingjian

The parting tune of Sunny Pass
   Melody finished, the river is still
      on the eastward running; beneath

Jingyang Mountain, a blaze of lights,
   and a leaf of boat. Tonight, I'll drink
      myself drunk, as always; a riverful

of crisp wind and bright moon seems
   to be sharing my departing sorrow.

想念的季節   林明理

飛吧，
三月的木棉，
哭紅了春天的眼睛。

飛吧，
風箏載著同一張笑臉，
心却緊緊抓住了線。

飛吧，
楓葉輕落溪底，
行腳已沒有風塵。

飛吧，
我們都把心門打開，
讓光明的窗照射進來。
飛吧，
螢火蟲，

藏進滿天星，我是
沉默的夜。

The Season of Yearning   Lin Ming-Li

Flying,
The cotton tree of March
Has wept red the eyes of spring.

Fly,
The kite carries the same smiling face,
When the heart firmly grasps the thread.

Fly,
Maple leaves fall gently down the bottom of the stream,
The footsteps are free from wind and dust.

Fly,
Let us open the door of our hearts,
To let in the bright light through the window.

Fly,
Glowworms,
Concealed in the maze of stars, I am
The silent night.

77．

題陽關圖二首（其一）   黃庭堅

斷腸聲裡無形影，畫出無聲亦斷腸。
想得陽關更西路，北風低草見牛羊。

Two Poems on the *Painting of the Sunny Pass* (1)
Huang Tingjian

The Sunny Pass Melody, a heart-
   breaking tune, is formless and
      traceless in the painting, but

silence speaks louder than voice:
   it is likewise captivating and heart-
      breaking. In the west of the west-

ward Sunny Pass, the chilly north
   wind bends the grass, to reveal
      flocks and herds of cows and sheep.

夜思
林明理

我愛北望──
冬日從扶桑樹頂
頂著暈環，堅韌地升起。
我愛
蒼穹下的紫薇。
愛那些熟悉的丹牆城台
大糖葫蘆，
我懷念
老張的大宅門口
夜裡挑擔兒的杏仁茶
那拐彎的館樓盡頭
一棵老槐樹
無數片雪花漫飄而落……
石橋前的琅琅聲忽近忽遠
呵，故國，呵，塵夢

除了潔淨是你的清碧
或者比白鷺身影更濃重。
驀然星子炯炯
直入我深情的瞳孔,
連風也斑駁。

## Night Thoughts	Lin Ming-Li

I'd like to look northward —
In winter atop the Mulberry tree
Against the faint circles, to rise up stubbornly
I love
The crape myrtle under the sky
And the familiar red walls and towers
Big sugar coated haws on a stick
I long for
The almond tea carried here at night
At the gate of Old Zhang's House
At the end of the building round the corner
An old Chinese scholar tree
Countless snowflakes are flying down….
Before the stone bridge the sound of reading from afar and near
Oh, homeland, oh, mortal dream
Except for cleanness as your pure green
Or heavier than the form of the egret
The stars twinkle all of a sudden
Into my passionate pupils
Even the wind is mottled

78 ·

到桂林   黃庭堅

桂嶺環城如雁蕩，平地蒼玉忽嶒峨。
李成不在郭熙死，奈此百嶂千峰何！

In Guilin   Huang Tingjian

The city of Guilin is encircled
   by Guiling Mountain which,
      taken a broad view, is like

a huge piece of green jade
   which rises abruptly out of
      the ground, towering. An

eternal pity — famous painters
   Li Cheng and Guo Xi have
      both passed away and, we

are helpless before myriads
   of peaks and valleys, which
      are piled with green upon green.

致摯友   林明理

我佇立於福爾摩沙
望穿中央山脈到大西洋
穿過海流和茂林
穿過巨石和礫灘
去追逐你奔馳的方向
我寄給你的信

是我小小的憂鬱
而你的容顏，璀璨明亮
彷彿黑暗中冉冉升起的太陽

To my best friend Lin Ming-Li

I stand in Formosa
Looking over the central mountains toward
the Atlantic Ocean
Through waves and dense forests
Through boulders and sand beaches
to follow your moving direction
My letter carries some of my melancholy
And your face, bright and brilliant
Is like the sun rising slowly from the dark

79.

雨中登岳陽樓望君山二首（其一）　　黃庭堅

投荒萬死鬢毛斑，生出瞿塘灩澦關。
未到江南先一笑，岳陽樓上對君山。

Watching Junshan Mountain Opposite Yueyang Tower in the Rain (No. 1 of 2 poems) Huang Tingjian

Exiled to the remote frontier,
　I have a narrow escape from
　　death, silver-streaked; it is a

miracle I can come back safe
   and sound, going through
      the dangerous Qutang Gorge.

Approaching the Southern Shore
   of my native land, I cannot
      help laughing; standing on

Yueyang Tower, I am gazing at
   the opposite Junshan Mountain,
      which is faintly visible.

靜湖   林明理

金陽下
碧湖上的天真
像是幻覺

整片雲杉林
醉人的綠
漂浮在欸乃間

問：
是否離開了時間
逝去的愛便
永不老謝？

是否沿著你的左岸
就能找得著
昔日的翠柳燕飛？

The Quiet Lake   Lin Ming-Li

Under the golden sunshine
The naivety over the blue lake

Like an illusion
The whole forest of spruce
Intoxicating green
Floating among the oaring & singing

Pray:
If without time
The departed love
Shall last for aye?

Along your left bank
Can the emerald willows and flying swallows
Of yore be found?

---

80 ·

雨中登岳陽樓望君山二首（其二） 黃庭堅

滿川風雨獨憑欄，綰結湘娥十二鬟。
可惜不當湖水面，銀山堆裡看青山。

Watching Junshan Mountain Opposite Yueyang Tower in the Rain (No. 2 of 2 poems)
Huang Tingjian

Leaning alone against the balustrade
  of Yueyang Tower, I am gazing
    at the lakeful of winds and rains,

through which looms the distant
  Junshan Mountain, seemingly like
    the legendary Lady Xiang whose

head is wearing twelve buns. It is
   a great pity that I cannot approach
      the water surface of Dongting Lake

so as to, over the perilous waves
   which are like silvery mountains,
      admire the blue Junshan Mountain.

寒風吹起 　　　　　　　　　　林明理

鬱鬱的，冬在怯怯萌芽
遠處幾聲犬號，擊破四周靜默
請聽，風的狂野曲調
草原都迷失在初雪中
在清曠的夜色
我想吟哦
浮光底下
多少尋尋覓覓的憧憬
恍然清醒
無聲的落入大海
波瀾也不起了
這鴻飛如旅人的，那裡來的
江南之雪啣
你或已忘記？請聽風在舞踴
當一切都靜止下來，卻盡夠使
我感到清寒，那無數的
瞬間，織就成綿密的鄉愁
向澄澄的明月，群山紛紛白頭

The Cold Wind Is Blowing　　Lin Ming-Li

Gloomily, winter is budding timidly
A few barks from afar, to break the walls of silence
Listen, the wild melody of wind

The grassland is lost in the first snow
In the vast purity of the night
I want to croon
Under the floating light
How many longings and yearnings
Sudden awakening
Voicelessly to fall into the sea
Without any waves
The geese in flight are like travelers, with
Snow in the south of the Yangtze River
Perhaps you have forgotten it?
Listen to the dancing wind
When everything comes to a stop, yet
I feel pure coldness, the countless
Moments, to be woven into heavy nostalgia
Toward the clear moon,
all the mountains are crowned white

81 ·

憶錢塘江　　　　　　　　　　　　　　李覯

昔年乘醉舉歸帆，隱隱前山半日銜。
好是滿江涵返照，水仙齊著淡紅衫。

In Remembrance of Qiantang River

Li Gou

When I board the sailing boat
　bound for my home, I am tipsy;
　　the two banks loom with blue

mountains, which have half
   devoured the setting sun. Most
      charming scene: a riverful of

reflected sunbeams lend a reddish
   hue to the dot after dot of white
      sails which, like a cluster after

another cluster of narcissus,
   are putting on red blouses.

四草湖中 　　　　　　　　　　　　　　　　　林明理

我聽過天空
嘎嘎這嘎嘎那的雷響,還有
消失卅餘年的鳥蚶重回四草湖懷抱
我歡喜,因為我知道寧靜
如這群白鷺
正緊跟著夕陽而且習以為常了
那紅樹林就在前方
映照出深淺不一的藍
不過,我喜愛的
不只是招潮蟹招展在泥灘
或是氣定神凝的彈塗魚
我關注的
其實只有復育的榮耀
我尋覓,再尋覓
嘎嘎這嘎嘎那的雷響,我用心觀察──
並沉湎於最遠那閃光的河道

In the Sicao Lake 　　　　　　　　Lin Ming-Li

I've heard of the sky
The thunder rumbling here and there, and

The birds and cockles which have disappeared for 30 years
are back to the lake
I am gladdened, because I know quietude
Like the flock of egrets
Following the setting sun as usual
The mangrove forest is ahead
To reflect different shades of blue
However, what I love
Is not only the fiddler crabs flaunting in the muddy beach
Or the calm and unperturbed mudskippers
What I care for
Is only the glory of restoration
I search and search
The thunder rumbling here and there,
I observe carefully —
Absorbed in the remotest glittering river

82 ·

鄉思 李覯

人言落日是天涯，望極天涯不見家。
已恨碧山相阻隔，碧山還被暮雲遮。

Homesickness Li Gou

It is said the spot where the sun
   sets is the horizon; and I look
     longingly beyond the horizon,

still my home is not in view.
    A great pity for me: hills upon
        hills have cut off the connection

between my home and me, and
    the endless hills are veiled
        by boundless murky clouds.

恬念   林明理

整個冬天
雪從沙路上銜起了
啼聲
春天
你是霧中羊
把我的回憶
搖成咽啞的頸鈴

遠方
綿綿山巒
拉曳出點點星辰
有棵樹仍挺立
慢慢
消融了我瘦骨的影

Solicitousness   Lin Ming-Li

The whole winter
The snow holds in mouth twitters
From the sandy road
The spring
You are a sheep in the fog

To shake my memory
Into toneless bells on the neck

Far away
Hills meander upon hills
To stretch dots after dots of stars
A tree is still standing
Slowly
To melt my lean form

---

83 ·

城南 　　　　　　　　　　　　　　曾鞏

雨過橫塘水滿堤，亂山高下路東西。
一番桃李花開盡，惟有青青草色齊。

The Southern Suburb　　　Zeng Gong

A torrential rain sweeps
   past the horizontal pool,
     and all dykes and dams

are overflowing with water;
   horizontal hills and vertical
     peaks, high and low, suddenly

east and suddenly west.
   Annual peach flowers and
     plum tree flowers: blossoming,

blossomed, fading, faded,
   when lushly green grass
      is still steadily growing.

山居歲月   林明理

一聲磬中洗騷魂，
   幾點霧雨迢曉月；
杏林徑裡有孤竹，
   晚課聲中看鳥飛。

Years in the Mountain   Lin Ming-Li

The sound of a chime stone my poetic soul is refreshed;
   A few drops of rain and the moon looms afar.
Solitary bamboos standing in the apricot grove,
   In evensongs I watch the birds wheeling and flying.

84 ·

宿濟州西門外旅館   晁端友

寒林殘日欲棲烏，壁裡青燈乍有無。
小雨愔愔人不寐，臥聽羸馬齧殘芻。

In a Hotel   Chao Duanyou

Woods of cold autumn,
   the sun is setting westward,
      crows returning to their nests;

a weak lamp in the niche
   of the wall, now dim and
     now bright. A fine rain

is drizzling noiselessly,
   when the wanderer is
     sleeplessly lying in his

bed, lending an ear to an
   old horse munching and
     chewing forage and fodder.

黃昏雨 　　　　　　　　　　　　　林明理

雨高懸在殿前
佔據著山頭
連綿到河岸匍匐在
綠蔭下，突然消失於下墜的夕陽中

因為來去匆匆
它的身影有鑲邊玻璃那麼亮
小時候我就是鏡裡的雪河
披上暈紅的新裝，等待花落

這場雨把院落靜得恍如出世
也帶來最驚喜的聲音
卻老聽見
自己的腳步踏在
石板面上的
回聲

Rain at Dusk 　　　　　　　　Lin Ming-Li

The rain curtain is hanging high before the temple
Occupying the mountaintop

Stretching to the river shore, crawling
Under the green shade, suddenly to disappear in the setting sun

Owing to hurried coming and leaving
Its form is as bright as a sheet of trimmed glass
As a child I was a snowy river in the mirror
Wearing new rosy clothes, waiting for the falling of flowers

The rain washes the yard into an ethereal one
With a pleasant voice
But always audible
My own footsteps
On the slabstone
Echoing

85 ·

曉齊 　　　　　　　　　　　　　　　司馬光

夢覺繁聲絕，林光透隙來。
開門驚烏鳥，餘滴落蒼苔。

A Fine Morning After the Night Rain
Sima Guang

Waking up from a nightlong
　sound sleep, I find thickly
　　falling rain let up; wisps

and beams of morning sun-
    shine reach me after penetrating
        forest leaves. Upon my

pushing open the door, crows
    and magpies are startled into
        a hurried flight, who shake

down from their branches
    drops of water on the green
        moss, splashing and spattering.

拂曉時刻 　　　　　　　　　　　　　　林明理

我們遇到迷霧
雖說還是冬季
湖塘微吐水氣
睫毛上也沾著露珠

細談中
一隻鷺在鏡頭前踟躕
這濕地森林
悄然褪色
萬物彷彿都在睡中

哪裡是野生天堂
如何飛離憂悒的白晝
我們啞然以對
只有小河隨心所願貌似輕鬆

At Daybreak 　　　　　　　　Lin Ming-Li

We are caught in a dense fog
Though it is still winter

The pond gently spitting up vapor
Dewdrops hang on the eyelashes

In casual chatting
An egret is hesitating before the camera lens
The wetland and forest
Is secretly fading away
As if myriads of things are asleep

Where is paradise for the wild
How to flee the sorrowful day
We are speechless for an answer
Only the brook seems to be easy and leisurely

86 ·

泗州東城晚望　　　　　　　　　秦觀

渺渺孤城白水環，舳艫人語夕霏間。
林梢一抹青如畫，應是淮流轉處山。

An Evening View at the Suburb　Qin Guan

A distant view: the lonely
   town is encircled with
     a white water; under the

foggy sun which is setting,
   whispering words are heard
     from the boat afloat on the

river. Beyond the treetops
there is a patch of dark
green which is picturesque

— it must be the bending
of Huai River, where
a crowd of hills gather.

問愛 　　　　　　　　　　　　　　　　　　　　林明理

在深不可測的眼神裡
我無法判斷
哪些是真實哪些是謊言

籃子裡的貓，瞇著眼
打了個呵欠
回答了所有的問題

牠懶洋洋地蹲伏於窗口
知道我無法逃遁

最後牠輕輕踱向我
彷彿愛情根本不存在過
除了這晦暗的雨中寧靜

About Love 　　　　　　　　　　　　　Lin Ming-Li

In the unfathomable eyes
I cannot judge
Which is truth and which is falsity

The cat in the basket is squinting
And yawning
And the question is answered

Crouching lazily by the window
Knowing that I have no way to escape
Gently it walks up to me
As if there is no such stuff of love
Except for the tranquility in the gloomy rain

---

87 ·

春日   秦觀

一夕輕雷落萬絲，霽光浮瓦碧參差。
有情芍藥含春淚，無力薔薇臥曉枝。

A Spring Day   Qin Guan

Last night, a slight thunder
 gives rise to myriads of
  filaments of rain, after which

the morning sun shines brilliantly
 on green glazed tiles. Peony
  flowers, sentimental, are watery

with teardrops; sickly roses,
 bathed in morning twilight,
  are spreading and sprawling.

冬之雪   林明理

說起北方
到底有多遠

讓你忍不住流下淚
回鄉路太長
只得把它折疊入夢
啊母親的手
從荊棘叢中向我伸來
撫摸著我苦楚的童年

Winter Snow Lin Ming-Li

Concerning the North
How far it is
You fail to check your tears
Too long is the homeward way
It has to be folded in the dream
Ah Mother's hands
Stretch to me from the thorns
Fondling my painful childhood

88．

秋日 秦觀

霜落邗溝積水清，寒星無數傍船明。
菰蒲深處疑無地，忽有人家笑語聲。

An Autumn Day Qin Guan

Frosty mornings, the water
　of Han Canal is transparently
　　limpid; a maze of stars

mirrored in water, twinkling
　　about the boat. The depth of
　　　reeds and cattail seems unpassable,

when suddenly family talking
　　is heard from nowhere.

寂靜蔭綠的雪道中 　　　　　　　　　林明理

在寂靜蔭綠的雪道中
風偷走了我的夢
它像小冠花對晶瑩的樹
把我心弦拋向雲層
這是怎樣的命運？無論
何處，都無法當成一首歌
在我褪去所有光輝的一刻
生命已無所求
啊……孤寂的十月
彷彿能看到你詩思篇篇
你是我懵懂歲月的樂聲
夜裡的海洋、聖壇的明燭
爾後，我將忘卻我的驕傲
在你轉身時綻出一絲焦灼
溶入花傘下
驟然聚凝的蒼穹

Along the Lonely and Green Shaded Snowy Path
　　　　　　　　　　　　　　Lin Ming-Li

Along the lonely and green shaded snowy path
The wind has stolen my dream
Which is like little crown flower against a glittering tree
The string of my heart is coaxed skyward into clouds

What kind of fate? No matter
Where, it cannot be taken as a song
The moment I shed off all my glory
In life there are no more desires
Ah…the lonely October
I seem to see your pieces from poetic thinking
You are the music in my innocent age
The sea of night, the candle on the altar
Then, I will forget my pride
When you turn round there will be a shade of anxiety
To dissolve under the umbrella
The vault of heaven which suddenly condenses

89 ·

金山晚眺   秦觀

西津江口月初弦，水氣昏昏上接天。
清渚白沙茫不辨，只應燈火是漁船。

An Evening View from the Golden Hill
Qin Guan

Over the estuary of West Ferry,
   a crescent moon shines bright;
     it is misty and vapory over

the river, water and the sky
   merging into one. The sandy
     islet is pure and clear, enveloped

in a stretch of whiteness; only
　　lamps are seen from afar,
　　　　which must be the fishing boats.

海影　　　　　　　　　　　　　　　林明理

第一次被你感動
我很難說清
在你燦爛的光痕
我以為世上並無如此美好的真情
是風的呼喚
讓我們因緣際會
想讓你認出了我
就忘了國與國的距離
有什麼差別

當我喜愛這一切──
棕櫚樹和沙灘、詩集
音樂
啊，島嶼一望無際
如何能留住你的身影
月亮啊，請不要再多說
我只信眼前所聞
一次相遇肯定不夠
在灰藍、灰藍的星群上
明天，請為我們打開希望之門

The Shadow of the Sea　　　Lin Ming-Li

The first time I was touched by you
The reason hard to name
In your brilliant traces

I don't think there is such a nice feeling
in the world
The calling of the wind
Makes us meet to be together
For you to know me
The distance between countries is forgotten
What is the difference
When I love all these —
Palm trees, sandy beach, poetry collections
Music
Ah, the island is boundless
How to keep your form
Oh, the moon, please say no more
I only believe what is before my eyes
One meeting is inadequate
Beyond the blue-gray constellation
Tomorrow, please open the door of hope for us

90 ·

禾熟 孔平仲

百里西風禾黍香，鳴泉落竇穀登場。
老牛粗了耕耘債，齧草坡頭臥夕陽。

Ripening Crops Kong Pingzhong

Autumn wind blows hundreds
   of miles, wafting with the scent
     of all crops; spring water is jingling

and trickling, when the threshing
　　ground is alive with various activities.
　　　　The labor of tilling and plowing

finished, the old cow, bathed in
　　the setting sun, is lying on the grassy
　　　　slope, munching and chewing grass.

憶夢　　　　　　　　　　　　　　　林明理

哪裡去尋找
一種聲音
像枝葉間接力的蟬
在廣場前
新穀還有漸次消失的
田，老農撩起褲管
種菜插秧

啊小小的火窗[18]
燃燒著希望
在溝岸旁
抓魚、游泳、釣蛙
油菜花和小雲雀嬉遊
街燈黯淡而溫暖

現在我知道
無論什麼季節
有一種聲音
像只蟹，眼裡還沾著細沙
就迫不及待往岸上爬
它牽引著我，在清蔭的夜晚

---

[18] 火窗又稱迷你烘爐〈火爐〉，在寒冬給老人家取暖用的。

Memory of a Dream   Lin Ming-Li

Where to look for
A voice
Like the cicadas engaged in a relay race in the leaves
Before the square
New grain and the gradually disappearing
Fields, the old farmer rolls up his trouser legs
To grow vegetables and plant seedlings

Ah, the little fiery window as a burner
Is burning with hopes
By the bank and ditch
To fish, swim, and catch frogs
Rape flowers and little larks are frolicking
Street lights are dim and warm

Now I know
Whatever the season
There is a voice
Like a crab, with fine sand in its eyes
It is impatient to climb onto the bank
It pulls me, in the cool night

91．

寄內   孔平仲

試說途中景，方知別後心。
行人日暮少，風雪亂山深。

To My Wife

Kong Pingzhong

The scenery along the way,
   I'll detail it to you; after
     separation from you, my

heart, to whom to bare?
   The dusk sun, being swallowed
     by the mountain, sees few

travelers; against a raging
   snowstorm, mountains multiply
     in riotous snowflakes and I,

alone on a long journey,
   a lone soul to be devoured
     by deep mountains.

無言的讚美

林明理

我和西天
追趕不上的雲朵
踏上這一片夢土

薩摩亞的藍湖初醒
雄奇而神秘
撲眼而來

山是以沉默　露出
蘋果也似的
笑容

Wordless Praise

Lin Ming-Li

The clouds with which the western sky
And I fail to catch up
Now is over this land of dream

The initial awakening of the Samoa' blue lake
Majestic and mysterious
Eye-catching

With its silence   the mountain reveals
Its smile
Like an apple

---

92 ·

村居

張舜民

水繞陂田竹繞籬，榆錢落盡槿花稀。
夕陽牛背無人臥，帶得寒鴉兩兩歸。

Village Life

Zhang Shunmin

Water is meandering in the
　　uneven field, green bamboos
　　　　surrounding the hedge; elm trees

are bare of clusters of seeds, and
　　shrub althea flowers are thinning
　　　　out. The setting sun sees nobody

on the cow back but pairs of
   crows sitting close to each
      other, on their homeward way.

夕陽，驀地沉落了 　　　　　　　林明理

夕陽，驀地沉落了
在魚鱗瓦上
在老厝的茶園旁
一片灰雲
躲入我衫袖
時常跟著我
一步步奔躍向前的
小河
加快了步子
臨近新丘

就這樣
從河而來
翻飛的記憶
恰似風鈴花開
雖然披紅那堪早落

The Setting Sun Sinks Down Suddenly
Lin Ming-Li

The setting sun sinks down suddenly
On the scaly tiles
By the old teahouse
A stretch of gray clouds
Hidden in my sleeves

Always following me
Running and leaping forward
The small river
Quickens its steps
Approaching the new hill

Thus
Coming from the river
The flying memories
Like the flowering of Campanula
Unbearable is the early falling in spite of wearing in red

93 ·

野步　　　　　　　　　　　　　　　　　　　　賀鑄

津頭微徑望城斜，水落孤村格嫩沙。
黃草庵中疏雨濕，白頭翁媼坐看瓜。

A Field Stroll　　　　　　　　　　　　He Zhu

At a ferry, a circuitous road
   leads to the town; with the
      falling tide, the solitary village

is enclosed with fine white
   sand. A persistently drizzling
      rain has drenched the thatched

hut, where a silver-streaked
   couple are still keeping
      guard of their melons.

小雨 　　　　　　　　　　　　　　　林明理

悄悄的回來了
似老僧入了定似的
閉目，一句也不說

偶爾
走在椅徑間彎著背
再停步，幾株薔薇竟熱望地開著
那一小撮的紅－
那是微笑的影子
掩映著她的臉如波鱗般的光

轉瞬間
只剩老樹叢上的行雲
低眉淺笑著，是小雨還是松風
老是吹我入兒時久遊的夢

Slight Rain 　　　　　　　　　Lin Ming-Li

Coming back quietly
Like an old monk in meditation
Eyes closed, nothing said

Occasionally
Walking along the path between chairs
with a bent back
Stop again, a few roses are flowering
That little cluster of red —
That is the shadow of a smile
To shade her face, like scaly light

In a flash
Only the clouds above the old trees remain

宋詩明理接千載
古今抒情詩三百首
漢英對照

Smiling lightly, is it the light rain or the pine wind
Always blowing me into the dream of my remote childhood
dream

94 ·

樓禪暮歸書所見二首（其一）　　　唐庚

雨在時時黑，春歸處處青。
山深失小寺，湖盡得孤亭。

Evening Return into the Zen Mountain (1)　　Tang Geng

The rain now starts and then
　　stops: it is still dark. With
　　　　the advent of spring, it is green

here, there, and everywhere.
　　Where the Zen Mountain towers,
　　　　the temple dwindles to disappear

from the view; at the end
　　of the lake water, a solitary
　　　　pavilion is standing by itself.

雨影　　　　　　　　　　　　　　林明理

山角之轉彎。於
古渡口的小鎮上

你
被風刮得
偏離了方向
突然　閃爍的電光
清晰地照出半面的
白髮
在樹影輕輕飄下
於午後
聽蟬鳴
於
一次次
蛻變之中
直到河水越來越急
你方驚醒：
雨還是雨，停在船頭
而晦暗下來的世界
已然重新點亮

The Shadow of Rain   Lin Ming-Li

The bend in the mountain. In
the small town near the ancient ferry
You
Are blown away
By the wind
Suddenly   a flash of lightning
Clearly illuminates half of
Your gray hair
Floating gently down from the tree shadow
In the afternoon
To listen to the chirping
Of cicadas
Time and again

In transformation
Until the river runs more and more rapidly
And you are awake
The rain is still the rain, stopping
at the bow of the boat
The darkened world
Is illuminated again

95 ·

樓襌暮歸書所見二首（其二）　　　唐庚

春到湖煙膩，晴搖野水光。
草青仍過雨，山紫更斜陽。

Evening Return into the Zen Mountain (2)

Tang Geng

Spring is here, and the lake
　is misty with heavy fog;
　　under brilliance of the sun,

running water in the field
　is bright with glittering and
　　twinkling beams. Washed

by spring rain, green grass
　is greener, dripping with green;
　　caught in the slanting sun,
　　　the mountain is all crimson.

曾經　　　　　　　　　　　　　　　　林明理

你輕俏得似掠過細石的
小溪，似水塘底白霧，揉縮
隨我步向籬柵探尋你的澄碧
我卻驟然顛覆了時空
熟悉你的每一次巧合

你微笑像幅半完成的畫
淨潔是你的幾筆刻劃，無羈無求
那青松的頌讚，風的吟遊：
誰能於萬籟之中盈盈閃動？每當
黃昏靠近窗口

今夜你佇立木橋
你的夢想，你的執著與彷徨
彷徨使人擔憂
惟有星星拖曳著背影，而小雨也
悄悄地貼近我的額頭

Once　　　　　　　　　　　　　Lin Ming-Li

You are light, like a stream running over
Pebbles, like the white mist at the pond bottom, kneading
To follow me to the fence in search of your clear blue
But suddenly I overturn time and space
To be familiar with each coincidence with you

Your smile is like a half-finished painting
Neatness is a few strokes by you, unrestrained,
to desire nothing
Praise of the green pine, chanting of the wind:

Who can flicker in myriads of things? Whenever
Dusk approaches the window

Tonight you stand on the wooden bridge
Your dream, your perseverance and hesitation
Hesitation brings worry
Only the stars are roving with their shadows,
and the drizzle
Also quietly approaches my forehead

96·

十七日觀潮　　　　　　　　　　　　陳師道

漫漫平沙走白虹，瑤台失手玉杯空。
晴天搖動清江底，晚日浮沉急浪中。

Watching Tide in Summer　　　Chen Shidao

Endlessly stretches the sandy
   bank which is white and flat;
     waves upon waves of surging

water are like the running white
   rainbow. It must be by a slip
     of hand, the heavenly immortal

has tilted his glass to empty
   out all the nectar, and the blue
     sky is waving and shaking

in the bed of the limpid river,
   and the evening sun, against
      strong winds and heavy waters,

is bobbing up and down,
   to appear and to disappear.

夜航 　　　　　　　　　　　　　林明理

是秋的臘染
紫雲，浪潮拍岸
是繁星
旋轉，還有萬重山

當夜敲著故鄉的門
小樓的風鈴就傳開了
那海河的橄欖林
在銀色的石徑裡醒來
被風起的流光
點出滿身晶瑩的背影

只有我於天幕下
仰望高空
在雨濕來臨前
趁著黑夜
飛越玉壁金川……

Night Navigation 　　　　　Lin Ming-Li

It is the tints of autumn
Purple clouds, waves lashing against the shore
It is the maze of stars
Spinning, and mountains upon mountains

When the night knocks on the native door
There are the wind chimes of the small building

The olive forest along the Haihe River
Wakes up in the silver stone path
The light blown by the wind
Twinkling with crystalline forms

Under the vault of heaven
Only I look up at the sky
Before the rain comes
Under the cover of the night
To fly over the jade wall and golden river……

97 ·

春遊湖　　　　　　　　　　　　　　徐俯

雙飛燕子幾時回？夾岸桃花蘸水開。
春雨斷橋人不度，小舟撐出柳陰來。

Spring Excursion to the Lake　　Xu Fu

A pair after another pair
　of swallows, when to fly
　　back? Two bankfuls of

blossoming peach flowers,
　dipping in the lake. Spring
　　drizzling, a bridge buried

in water to obstruct the passage,
> when a boat steals out of the
>> shade of willow twigs.

春已歸去 　　　　　　　　　　　　　　林明理

不知不覺間
托著嫩綠帶毛的小桃子
又一次，向我訴說著
一種心事
蕭蕭沙沙
麥子枯黃了
榆樹的殘花停留在四月
風總是微微的
甜甜的吹
時時送來的布穀鳥的叫聲
也沒有變
春已遠去
籬笆外包圍著
一塊古老的桑田
荷葉一片二片……
浮泛在水面
而陽光正好暖和
向牆上雨痕悄然走過

Vanished Spring 　　　　　　　　Lin Ming-Li

Unconsciously
Holding the small peaches of tender green with hair
Again, you tell me
About your frame of mind
Rustling and whistling
The wheat ripens to be yellow

The withered elm flowers linger in April
The wind blows gently
And sweetly
From time to time it carries the cawing of cuckoos
Which remains unchanged
Vanished is spring
Beyond the fence
There is a stretch of age-old field
One or two lotus leaves….
Floating on the water
So warm is the sunlight
Quietly a trace of rain on the wall

98 ·

聞笛 　　　　　　　　　　　　　　　劉吉甫

戍鼓停撾月五更，嗚嗚巧作斷腸聲。
江南自是春來早，吹到梅花夢也清。

Hearing the Fluting　　　　　　　　Liu Jifu

The garrison drum
   stops at the fifth watch
      of night, when the fluting

sound is heart-breaking.
   Spring springs early
      south of the Yangtze

River, and through plum
 blossoms, it is melodious
 in my pure dream.

春風,流在百草上 　　　　　林明理

如果妳在獨自歸來的小路
偶然低首
只這一瞬間
我也會在樹旁
用彩蝶的青綠紅黃
跟著紫花飛舞起來
直到樹影倒在籬笆上
讓妳輕輕地拍著湖水
重新拂動——
妳比青青的柳絲還要瀟灑
比一方小石還要潔淨
而枝上的雀兒
也唱出我們心中的歌
如果妳在獨自歸來的小路
趁著紅雲還在天邊
我也在靜睡的
小樹下哼著
等妳轉身
我已消失在
遠天的暮色

Spring Wind Flowing Over Grasses
　　　　　　　　　　　Lin Ming-li

On the path of your solitary returning
Occasionally to bow your head
For the moment
Beside the tree I will

Follow the purple flowers in flight
With the blue, green, red, and yellow of colorful butterflies
Until the shadow of the tree falls on the fence
For you to gently beat the lake water
To brush it anew —
You are more graceful than green willows
More clean than a small stone
And the sparrows in the branches
Sing the song in our hearts
On the path of your solitary returning
If you take the advantage of red clouds still at the edge of the sky
I am sound asleep
Humming a tune under a small tree
When you turn around
I have disappeared in
The twilight of the distant sky

---

99 ·

九絕為亞卿作（其一） 韓駒

君住江濱起畫樓，妾居海角送潮頭。
潮中有妾相思淚，流到樓前更不流。

Nine Quatrains Composed When Touched by the Love Story of My Friend (1)
Han Ju

You live in a seaside
  painted house, and I
    live in the horizon,

facing from day to day
   the surging waves of
      the sea, where my tears

of yearning for you are
   mixed, running to stop
      in front of your house.

瓶中信　　　　　　　　　　　　　　林明理

緊抱僅有的一線
希望，寄託波浪
她傳遞的使命，
支撐著夢想。

風霜的臉　佈滿了驟雨，
強忍著痛。
一座冰山　擋在她的胸口，
請求通航。

風知道她來自古老的故鄉
歷經萬險
只為一個不變的諾言，
像一個月亮。

Bottled Message　　　　　　　Lin Ming-Li

Holding on to the only ray
Of hope, entrusting it to the waves;
The mission conveyed by her
Supports my dreams.

Her weathered face　suggestive of rainstorm,
And the pain is endured.

An iceberg blocks in her chest,
Begging for navigation.

The wind knows she is from an ancient hometown,
Through myriads of dangers,
For an unalterable promise,
Like a moon.

---

100 ·

九絕為亞卿作（其二）   韓駒

妾願為雲逐畫檣，君言十日看歸航。
恐君回首高城隔，直倚江樓過夕陽。

Nine Quatrains Composed When Touched by the Love Story of My Friend (2)

Han Ju

How I wish to become
  a blossom of white cloud,
    to follow the painted boat;

but you tell me that you'll
  return in ten days, and no
    worry. Still I'm afraid, when

you turn back to look at me,
  your gaze will be obstructed
    by the tall walls of the town;

I climb atop the riverside tower,
   from day to day, to watch the
      setting sun slanting westward.

晚秋 　　　　　　　　　　　　　　林明理

在一片濃綠的陡坡
白光之下和風，把高地淅淅吹著。
妳回首望，淡淡的長裙
弄散滿地丁香。
我看見
花瓣掉落山城垂楊
晨霧漸失。雲雀
驚動了松果，妳淺淺一笑
彷彿世界揚起了一陣笙歌，
而笙歌在妳的四周
有無法不感到讚歎的奇趣。
今夜，
月已悄默，
只要用心端詳
石階草露也凝重
妳離去的背影催我斷腸
就像秋葉搖搖欲墜
又怎抵擋得住急驟的風？

Late Autumn 　　　　　　　　Lin Ming-Li

Along a steep slope which is darkly green
The gentle breeze under white light, to blow the highland.
You look back, in long, light skirt
To scatter scent of lilacs all over the ground.
I see

Petals falling, the mountain city veiled in weeping willows
Morning mist on the disappearing. Skylarks
Startle pine cones, and you smile slightly
As if the world is vocal with piping songs,
The songs are about you
An interest which solicits sighs and admiration.
Tonight,
The moon is silent,
So long as you gaze with care
The dew on stone steps is heavy
Your departing form renders me heartbroken
Like autumn leaves on the falling
How to resist the tempestuous wind?

101.

三衢道中 曾幾

梅子黃時日日晴，小溪泛盡卻山行。
綠陰不減來時路，添得黃鸝四五聲。

Along the Way   Zeng Ji

When plums ripen to be yellow,
   it is the rainy season, but a fine
     day after another fine day;

boating to the end of the river,
   I begin to walk in the mountain.
     Along the way, green greets

the eye, lush trees and green
   grass far and wide; in sheer
      quietude, orioles are twittering,

producing four or five more
   notes than the way otherwise.

頌黃梅挑花[19] 　　　　　　　林明理

我嚮往在黃梅鎮
鄰近名寺裡的那片樂土
   那兒的挑花工藝
是代代相傳的婦女作品
   已發展了五百年歷史
它美得像一首抒情詩
   讓我內心溢滿幸福

In Praise of Yellow Plum Cross-cut[20]
Lin Ming-Li

I long for the promised land near the famous temple
Near the Yellow Plum Town
   The cross-cut there

---

[19] 收到湖北省黃梅縣文化館鄭衛國館長寄贈一條黃梅挑花巾及詩集，很開心。黃梅挑花被列入中國大陸第一批國家級非物質文化遺產名錄的民間藝術，而鄭衛國主編過《黃梅挑花》的書。—2017.8.21

[20] I am delighted to receive a cross-cut scarf and a collection of poems from Zheng Weiguo, director of the Huangmei County Cultural Center in Hubei Province. the cross-cut embroidery is listed as a folk art in the first batch of national intangible cultural heritage lists in mainland China, and Zheng Weiguo is the editor of a book entitled *Yellow Plum Cross-cut.* –August 21, 2017.

Is the work of women passing down from generation to generation
    Boasting a history of 500 years
It is as beautiful as a lyrical poem
    Which fills my heart with happiness

102 ·

春日即事   李彌遜

小雨絲絲欲網春,落花狼藉近黃昏。
車塵不到張羅地,宿鳥聲中自掩門。

A Dusk in Spring   Li Mixun

The fine drizzle is like a thick-set
    net, seemingly to net spring, when
        a groundful of flowers are caught

and lit in the gathering dusk. The
    world is noisy with wheels which
        are rolling with rising dust, but few

visitors here, a secluded place; before
    a good night, I close my gate and my
        door, to shut out twitters of the birds.

歌飛阿里山森林   林明理

我穿過白髮的
阿里山林鐵
去尋覓童年的天真

這山泉
是個愛唱歌的小孩
音色細而堅韌
神木旁　還藏有
遊客們笑聲

當火車汽笛吶喊出
嘹亮的清音
風的裙步跟著踏響了冬林
土地的記憶
也化成一片片寧靜

我把縷縷陽光剪下
鐫刻在櫻樹上
它竟輕輕地
輕輕地
挽住了夕陽的金鬍子

啊，還有那雲海
從何時
已網住了我每一立方的夢境

Songs Fill the Forest of Mt. Ali

Lin Ming-Li

Through the forest iron of Mt. Ali
Which is gray-haired
I look for my childish innocence

The mountain spring
Is a child who loves singing
In a reedy and tenacious tone

Near divine trees　　hidden also
Is the laughter of travelers

When the train whistle produces
A loud and clear voice
The winter forest rings with the skirt steps of wind
The memory of land
Also turns into a piece after another piece of tranquility

Cutting down a beam after another beam of sunshine
I carve it on the cherry tree
And gently
Very gently
It catches the golden beard of the setting sun

Ah, the sea of clouds
Unawares
Has caught each cube of my dreamland in its net

---

103 ·

襄邑道中　　　　　　　　　　　　陳與義

飛花兩岸照船紅，百里榆堤半日風。
臥看滿天雲不動，不知雲與我俱東。

All the Way Down the River　　Chen Yuyi

My boat is red from two
　　bankfuls of flowers which
　　　　are wheeling and flying; the

riverbank, meandering for
   hundreds of miles, is overgrown
      with elm trees. For the better part

of the day I am bathed in spring
   wind and, lying in the boat, I find
      the sky filled with motionless

clouds, without knowing they
   are actually pursuing an eastward
      course, following my boat and me.

永懷星雲大師[21]   林明理

今夜,繁星中的您
像白鷺飛向湖邊
在皎潔的殿宇裡
超凡而欣喜——

您的話語
有禪悅中的慈悲
落在喜樂國亮閃的
花朵和朝露上,
都如此自然

仰望您——心懷眾生
為弘法所付出的慷慨
在十萬億土之外
必有您崇高的光芒

---

[21] 星雲大師(1927-2023),出生於江蘇省江都一個純樸的農家,出家後,信奉佛祖,決志弘法,不遺餘力,其願力堪與日月爭輝。他奉獻一生,無悔無私,享年九十七歲。僅以此詩對大師表達最深切的追思與敬意。

Eternal Memory of Master Hsing Yun[22]

Lin Ming-Li

Tonight, in the maze of stars
Like a white egret, you fly to the lake
In the bright temple
Extraordinary and joyful —

Your words
Have the compassion of Zen
Falling on the sparkling flowers
And morning dew in the Land of Bliss,
So naturally

Looking up to you — solicitous about all living beings
The generosity you have given to spreading the Dharma
Beyond trillions of lands
There must be your noble light

104·

初夏

朱淑真

竹搖清影罩幽窗，兩兩時禽噪夕陽。
謝卻海棠飛盡絮，困人天氣日初長。

---

[22] Master Hsing Yun (1927-2023) was born in a common farmer's family in Jiangdu, Jiangsu Province. After becoming a monk, he believes in Buddha and is determined to spread the Dharma with all his efforts. His wish is as brilliant as the sun and the moon. He has dedicated his life without regrets and dies at the age of ninety-seven. I would like to express my deepest remembrance and respect for the master through this poem.

The Early Summer   Zhu Shuzhen

Emerald bamboos are waving
   in the gentle wind, casting
      clear patterns on the quiet

window; birds, in pairs, are
   noisily chirping and twittering
      in the setting sun. Crab-apple

flowers are fading and withering,
   nearly no more dancing of
      willow catkins; with the advent

of summer, the days are
   lengthening and languishing.

夏日慵懶的午後   林明理

有座被鳥雀和
蓮花簇擁的小森林，
湖面似透鏡，
雲終於落下來。
我踮起腳尖，
按下快門的一瞬，
細碎的陽光是背景，
天空無語，卻令我沉迷。
我以為自己可以及時
找到真理和歡樂，
那遺世的孤獨
已離開很遠；
風總是靜靜地吹，
在這夏日慵懶的午後。

This Lazy Summer Afternoon

Lin Ming-Li

There is a small forest
Infested by birds and lotus flowers.
The lake surface is like a mirror;
The clouds eventually fall down.
I stand on tiptoe,
The moment I press the shutter of my camera,
The fine rays of sunlight as the background,
I am enthralled by the wordless sky.
I believe that I can find
Truth and joy in time;
The world-abandoning loneliness
Has been away for long;
The wind always blows gently,
In this lazy summer afternoon.

---

105 ·

除夜自石湖歸苕溪（其二）　　　姜夔

黃帽傳呼睡不成，投篙細細激流冰。
分明舊泊江南岸，舟尾春風颭客燈。

Going Home from the Stone Lake On New Year's Eve (2)

Jiang Kui

The yellow-capped boatmen
　are talking loudly to each other,
　　preventing the sleepy man from

dropping asleep; the boat bamboo
   into water, to gently touch and
      crack the thin film of ice. My

memory remains fresh: this is
   the very bank of the Southern
      Shore where we have ever anchored

in some night: spells after spells
   of spring wind blowing the
      lamp at the stern to be flickering.

我願是隻小帆船   林明理

我願是隻小帆船
　　　停靠在落霞外
每一次與大海相遇
　　　便興起絲絲回憶
若是雨飄下來
　　　孤獨不時出現時
我就那樣歌著……
　　　……給自己聽
是否我也只是在生活
　　　卻看不清生活是什麼
所有浪花都在低吟
所有星辰閃亮
我卻一直思念——
　　　莿桐花開了
還有從遠方
輾轉傳來的故事
是啊，無論我航行多久
家　　有多遠

在我心中，仍保留著一種愛
它　讓我時時回到故鄉
　　溫柔而寬廣的懷抱

I Wish I Were a Small Sailboat

Lin Ming-Li

I wish I were a small sailboat
　　　Mooring beyond the sunset
Each encounter with the sea
　　　There are lingering memories
If the rain falls down
　　　When loneliness visits from time to time
I sing like that……
　　　……To myself
Am I just living my life
　　　Without seeing clearly what life is
All the waves are humming
All the stars are shining
But I keep yearning —
　　　The tung flowers are blooming
And there are stories
Coming from afar
Yes, no matter how long I sail
How far　is home
In my heart, there is a kind of love
Which often brings me back to my hometown
　　　The gentle and massive embrace

橫溪堂春曉　　　　　　　　　　　　虞似良

一把青秧趁手青，輕煙漠漠雨冥冥。
東風染盡三千頃，白鷺飛來無處停。

A Spring Morning　　　　　　　　　Yu Siliang

Planted into water are a hand-
　ful of green rice sprouts which,
　　　charmed by the hands of the

farmer, are greener, against
　the gray background of a thin
　　　film of wafting mist from

the drizzling rain. The genial
　east wind has greened three
　　　thousand hectares of boundless

paddy field, where a bevy of
　white egrets in hesitant flight
　　　fail to find a landing or footing.

觀白鷺　　　　　　　　　　　　　　林明理

他垂下了翅羽
立於水面的岩石中
就這樣巍然不動──
彷若沉思的天使
任蜻蜓在頭上盤旋

一群野鴨款款游過
按下快門的那一瞬
我的心在雨後的校園微笑
泛著一種簡單的幸福

An Egret
                                Lin Ming-Li

He drops his wings
Standing on a rock in water
Thus motionless —
Like an angel in meditation
In spite of dragonflies circling above his head
A bevy of mallards swimming by
The instant the shutter is pressed
My heart is smiling in the campus after rain
Brimming with simple happiness

107·

早作二首（其一）
                                裘萬頃

井梧飛葉送秋聲，籬菊緘香待晚晴。
斗柄橫斜河欲沒，數山青處亂鴉鳴。

View of an Autumn Morning (1)
                                Qiu Wanqing

The well-side parasol tree
  begins to shed its leaves,
    spreading the sound of autumn

in the west wind; scent is
　　contained in hedge-side
　　　　chrysanthemums, not to diffuse

until it lets up in the evening.
　　The Big Dipper dips aslant
　　　　and the Milky Way is on the

disappearing, when the depth
　of a few blue peaks afar is
　　　　noisy with the twitters of crows.

我要回到從前　　　　　　　　　　林明理

我要回到從前
然後——
讓時間在那裡用夕陽織成
雲海，比夕陽更美的
是目所能見的瞬間

那守望著最心痛的臉
在暮色底下
我的思念啊！……
忽而從旁流過
去了又來

沒人能說
這一切是容易的
世界多變
靠近我的波影
一直在水天之間迴旋

I Want to Be Back to the Past Lin Ming-Li

I want to be back to the past
Then —
For time there to weave the setting sun into
A sea of clouds, more spectacular than the setting sun
Is the moment which can be seen

The face that watches the sharpest heartache
Under twilight
Oh my yearning! ……
Suddenly flowing by
Away to be back again

No one can say
All this is easy
The world is changeable
Approaching my waving form
Constantly turning between water and the sky

108・

秋齋即事　　　　　　　　　　　　　　　　　　　許棐

桂香吹過中秋了，菊傍重陽未肯開。
幾日銅瓶無可浸，賺他饑蝶入窗來。

My Study in Autumn   Xu Fei

Sweet osmanthus flowers
  are sweet no more after
    mid-autumn; the Double

Ninth Festival is around the
  corner, still chrysanthemums
    are reluctant to blossom.

For quite a number of days
  the copper vase is empty
    of fresh flowers, when a

butterfly thirsting for
  flowers flies, from the
    window, into my study.

穿過無數光年的夢   林明理

在思想的海洋裡
我想像愛情是何面貌
於是，我對星空發出訊號
但回聲如同細雪
飄飄蕩蕩，我，愈深想望它的模樣了

The Dream Through Countless Light Years
Lin Ming-Li

In the ocean of thought
I imagine the way of love
So, I send a message to the starry sky
But the echo is like fine snow
Drifting and floating, and I am keener about its way

109.

夜歸 　　　　　　　　　　　　　　　　　周密

夜深歸客依筇行，冷磷依螢聚土塍。
村店日昏泥徑滑，竹窗斜漏補衣燈。

Night Return 　　　　　　　　　Zhou Mi

The depth of night sees a
　homeward returnee, walking
　　with the support of a bamboo

stick; blue phosphorus and
　cold glowworms, bits and
　　dots, gathering over the low

banks of earth between fields.
　In the village a shop is vaguely
　　silhouetted, to which a muddy

and slippery road leads and,
　onward, from among the bamboo
　　woods appears a window, which

is dimly lit with a lamp, as well
　as a form mending clothes by it.

母親的微笑 　　　　　　　　　　　林明理

比一切更美的是您病癒之際
白色天空，小花草，竹籬笆

以及您髮間的淡雲朵
這些影像始終明亮而清晰
我在風聲與塵土中
輕駕著星星
朝向紅色的大橋
朝向故鄉的田疇
您在稻浪中笑了
黃昏把我們帶向極遠處

喔，母親
我最親愛的
因您，我獲得我要求的真理與愛
您的手心，宛如冬陽
投射出幸福的花田
而蹣跚的步履
依舊在我血液中湧動
往日，您是我的驕傲
如今，我闊步向前
把盼望已久的您的微笑迎進門來

Mother's Smile Lin Ming-Li

What is more beautiful than anything is when you are recovering from your illness
White sky, small flowers and grass, bamboo fence
And the light clouds in your hair
The images are constantly bright and clear
In the wind and dust
I am riding the stars
Toward the red bridge
Toward the field of my hometown
You smile in the rice waves
Dusk takes us far away

Oh, mother
My dearest
Owing to you, I get the truth and love which I need
Your palm is like the winter sun
Projecting the flowery field of happiness
The faltering steps
Still flowing in my blood
In the past you are my pride
Now, I stride forward
To welcome your long-awaited smile into the room

110．

雷峰夕照 尹廷高

煙光山色淡溟濛，千尺浮屠兀倚空。
湖上畫船歸欲盡，孤峰猶待夕陽紅。

Leifeng Pagoda Caught in the Sunset

Yin Yangao

Mist-light mixed with mountain
   color, all is veiled in a thin fog;
     looking from afar, the thousand-

feet tall Leifeng Pagoda is still
   standing and towering in the
     boundless sky. On the West Lake

which is rippling with green waves,
   one after another painted boat
     disappears, when the pagoda,

like a lonely proud peak, is still
　　waiting, with great patience,
　　　　to be caught in the sunset.

愛，是無可比擬的　　　　　　　　　林明理

愛，是無可比擬的
任何語言都難以形容
苦澀的愁緒
困窘的淚水
或假裝自己已從桎梏中逃脫
再也無所謂的謊言

世上沒有比愛更純粹的東西
卻讓世人一再詠讀它的篇章
一個淡淡的微笑或一個吻
便讓周圍嚮起了歌聲
但一旦面對挑戰
卻免不了驚慌失措

那便是愛了，它就像
隕落的天使重歸天際
那便是在朗朗月光下
每個人心中的星星
那便是可以讓你永遠回憶
永遠感受到的輕盈翩翩

Incomparable Is Love　　　　　　Lin Ming-Li

Incomparable is love
It is hard to describe in any language
The bitter sorrow

Tears of embarrassment
Or to pretend to have rid of the shackles
The lie that counts no more

The world boasts nothing purer than love
Yet the worldlings read and reread its chapters
A gentle smile or a kiss
And there is singing all about
Facing the challenges
Inevitable panic

This is love; it is like
The fallen angel back to the sky
Under the bright moonlight
The stars in everybody's heart
For you remember forever
And to feel forever the gentle winging

111 ·

淯淯 　　　　　　　　　　　　　　　王令

淯淯輕雲弄落暉，壞簷巢滿燕來歸。
小園桃李東風後，卻看楊花自在飛。

Flimsy Clouds 　　　　　　　　Wang Ling

Toward evening, the flimsy
　clouds are gently rising,
　　to play with beams of the

setting sun; under the broken
   eaves birds' nests throng and
      swarm, waiting for their return

for the night. The garden is
   riotous with peach flowers
      and plum tree flowers fading

and flying in the east wind,
   with the follower of poplar
      filaments, flying freely with ease.

AI 的世界將到來   林明理

1.
當 AI 迅速地擴展,
國與國之間的戰鼓,
也在夜裡一聲又一聲敲響。

2.
一架架無人機,沉浮著,
測量月球的距離,
探索火星是什麼世界?

3.
好戰的人類啊,
AI 或許會變成兇器,
變成太空競賽的手段。

4.
我能看見 AI 成為先進之國的象徵,
卻聽不清秋風對我聲訴些什麼。

宋詩明理蹉千載
古今抒情詩三百首 漢英對照

5.
只有北斗七星不厭其煩地
昭告人間,
回聲直落我的腳前。

6.
是的,在 AI 的角力中,
我回眸看飛雪中使勁地開出的一朵梅
衝破四周的黑影。

7.
我揣想,
外星世界也有這樣璀璨的白梅嗎?

8.
我揣想,天外的世界
與未來 AI 的世界之間,
是否仍有萬物滋長和顏色?

9.
或許 AI 發展的結局
並不盡然都一樣圓滿,
但列強已不可能鳴金收兵了。

10.
而我相信,
比人類更勇武的力量是「詩」,
把自己唱老了,就是天堂。

The World of AI Is Around the Conner
Lin Ming-Li

1.
When AI spreads quickly,
The war drums from country to country,
Are ringing from night to night.

2.
One after another unmanned aerial vehicle, floating and sinking,
To measure the distance to the moon,
To explore the unknown world of Mars.

3.
Oh trigger-happy people,
AI may become the weapon,
The means of Space Race.

4.
I can see AI as the emblem of advanced countries,
But I fail to make out the whispers of the autumn wind.

5.
Only the Big Dipper is tirelessly
Announcing to the world,
The echo falls straight by my feet.

6.
Yes, in the wrestle of AI,
I glance back at a plum blossom blossoming against the snow with efforts,
Breaking through the shadow all about.

7.
I ponder,
Whether there are so brilliantly white plum blossoms in the Alien World?

8.
I ponder, between the world beyond heaven
And the future world of AI,
Still myriads of things growing with various colors?

9.
Perhaps the end of the development of AI
Is not necessarily so satisfactory,
But it is impossible for the big powers to blow the retreat.

10.
And I believe,
Poetry is more powerful and brave than human beings,
It is paradise when you sing yourself into an old age.

112 ·

浪花　　　　　　　　　　　　　　　　王宷

一江秋水浸寒空，漁笛無端弄晚風。
萬里波心誰折得？夕陽影裡碎殘紅。

Sprays　　　　　　　　　　　　　　Wang Shen

A riverful of autumn water
　　seems to be steeped in the
　　　　cold air; the evening wind

is wafting with fishing fluting,
   traveling here to taper off.
      Sprays are twinkling in the

center of the boundless waves
   upon waves: who can pick
      them? In the setting sun,

sprays scatter and shatter
   into crimson patches and pieces.

在一片沙海中（組詩）　　　　林明理

1.
夕陽將落盡。
大翅鯨，歌聲在沙海上——
不停迴響。

2.
一隻豹，巡邏著。
小兔驚怯地把身子
鑽入岩縫。

3.
海龜揹著我
在阿曼[23]的柔波上，
瞅見阿拉伯半島之心。

4.
珊瑚礁的巨影……

---

[23] 阿曼蘇丹國（The Sultanate of Oman），簡稱：阿曼，西非國家。

變成個皇宮。
月亮在相望。

5.
石灰岩的懸崖,
羊和土狼活動的窄徑。
噢,萬物存在,絕非偶然。

6.
這片原生沙海,
跟聖經裡的黃金城、碧玉牆,
一樣珍貴,惹我懷想。

At a Sandy Sea (group poems) Lin Mingli

1.
The setting sun is to fade out.
A big-finned whale is singing at a sandy sea —
Keeping echoing.

2.
A leopard is patrolling.
A little rabbit turns around timidly
And gets itself into a rock crevice.

3.
The turtle is carrying me
On the soft waves of Oman[24],
To see the heart of Arabian Peninsula.

---

[24] The Sultanate of Oman, simplified as Oman, is a country in West Africa.

4.
The giant shadow of the coral reef....
Turns into a palace.
The moon is fondly looking.

5.
The cliffs of limestone,
Narrow trails for sheep and coyotes.
Oh, the existence of all things is no accidental.

6.
This native sandy sea
Is as precious as the golden city and jasper wall
In the Bible: it makes me miss you.

113．

黯淡院　　　　　　　　　　　　　　賈青

溪聲灘外急，草色雨中深。
客意自南北，山光無古今。

The Gloomy Courtyard　　　Jia Qing

The torrential water in
   the river beach is speeding
      and gurgling; the emerald

grass is greener in drizzling
   rain. Like birds of passage,
      the wanderers are wandering

aimlessly; the beauty of the
　landscape of mountains and
　　rivers and lakes retains as of old.

大堡礁彼岸[25]　　　　　　　　　　　林明理

1.
一對軍艦鳥
飛呀，竊取了孵卵。
海盜的圖像。

2.
剛產卵的母龜
在前灘來來去去，
如與死神交戰。

3.
大堡礁中，萬物繁衍。
海岸河川裡的水鱷，
是最高統治者。

4.
羽毛有毒刺，
海底世界裡，獅子魚
像高明的獵人。

5.
風起雲湧，
生命的脆弱與神聖，
像海蛇……
在珊瑚迷宮裡　穿梭。

---

[25] 大堡礁（英語：Great Barrier Reef）是世界最大最長的珊瑚礁群，位於澳洲。

6.
透骨的風，
在夜裡穿過雷恩島，
穿過剛剛甦醒的
花和冰河。

7.
在黑暗的深海，
希望是勇者的力量，
人類亦然。

Beyond the Great Barrier Reef[26]

Lin Ming-Li

1.
A pair of frigate birds
Flying, to steal the hatching eggs.
Pirate image.

2.
The female turtle who has newly laid eggs
Coming and going on the foreshore,
As if fighting with Death.

3.
In the Great Barrier Reef, myriads of things thrive.
Water crocodiles in coastal rivers,
Is the supreme ruler.

4.
Feathers have venomous spines,
In the underwater world, lionfish
Is like a skilled hunter.

---

[26] The Great Barrier Reef is the largest and the longest coral reef group in the world, which is located in Australia.

5.
The wind is surging,
The fragility and sanctity of life,
Like a sea snake…
Travels through the coral maze.

6.
The bone-piercing wind,
Passing the Isle of Wren at night,
Through the freshly awakened
Flowers and glaciers.

7.
In the dark, deep sea,
Hope is the strength of the brave,
It is the same with humans.

114 ·

花院 趙與滂

拆了秋千院宇空，無人楊柳自春風。
薔薇性野難拘束，卻過鄰家屋上紅。

A Flowery Courtyard — Zhao Yupang

Away with the swing,
  the courtyard is empty;
    willow branches are dancing

by themselves in spring
  wind. Wild by nature,
    wild roses are hard to tame:

rambling and sprawling
　over the neighboring roof,
　　they are flaming red.

夏日已逝　　　　　　　　　　　林明理

再見，炫目的夏日！
你最後與群星結伴嬉遊
讓我把世界拋諸腦後……
那身影，已在風中消逝了。

木荷花開燦爛，
那簇浪而起的深藍星河，
是你顧盼的回眸，
還是隨之飄轉的夢？

再見，我的微風！
你覆蓋又半透明的秘密，
如閃現的夜鶯，而展翼的
歌聲，也漸行漸遠了。

Summer Is Gone　　　　　　　Lin Ming-Li

Adieu, dazzling summer!
Eventually you travel with the stars
And I leave the world behind….
That form has disappeared in the wind.

The wood lotus blossoms brilliantly,
The deep blue galaxy with clusters of waves,
Is your backward glance,
Or a dream drifting with it?

Adieu, my breeze!
Your covered yet translucent secret,
Like a flashing nightingale, and the winged
Songs have also drifted away.

115.

題畫 　　　　　　　　　　　　　　　　　　李唐

雲裡煙村雨裡灘，看之容易作之難。
早知不入時人眼，多買燕脂畫牡丹。

On Painting 　　　　　　　　　　　　　　Li Tang

Villages enveloped
　in mist and fog, river
　　beaches caught in rain,

easy looking and difficult
　painting. If I know
　　this kind of works

do not cater to public
　taste, I would use the
　　paint to draw peonies.

淵泉 　　　　　　　　　　　　　　　　　　林明理

涼晨中
我聽見流泉就在前方
彷若一切拂逆與困厄
全都無懼地漂走

一隻信鴿在白樺樹林頻頻
投遞
春的祭典

我相信悲傷的愛情
它隨著蒼海浮光
有時擱淺在礁岸
隨沙礫嘎啦作響

The Deep Spring　　　　　　　　Lin Ming-Li

A cold morning
I hear a flowing spring ahead
As if all frustrations and distresses
Are floating away fearlessly

In the woods birches from time to time a white dove
Brings about
The sacrifices of spring

I believe in sorrowful love
It drifts along with the shimmering sea
Sometimes piling up on the shore
Making a harsh noise like grains of stone

116．

春遊吟　　　　　　　　吳沆

鳥語煙光裡，人行草色中。
池邊各分散，花下複相逢。

Spring Outing

Wu Hang

Birds' twitters travel
　through misty light and
　　smoky flowers, when

wanderers are wandering
　in green grass and verdure.
　　This moment separating

by the pool, the next
　moment get-together
　　among a riot of flowers.

記夢

林明理

一整晚妳的聲音如細浪
泛白了黯淡的星河
我匆匆留下一個吻
在滴溜的霧徑上
或者，也想出其不備地說
愛，其實笨拙如牛

現在我試著親近妳　給妳
一季的麥花，著實想逗引妳
深深地在手心呼吸一下
如貓的小嘴唱和著相酬的
詩譜，叫我聞得到
那逃逸的形跡是多麼輕盈
——漫過山后

Recalling a Dream Lin Ming-Li

Throughout the night your breath is like gentle waves
Whitening the darkish river of stars
In a hurry I leave behind a kiss
On the path heavily foggy
Or, want to say beyond expectation
Love, actually is awkward like an ox.

Now I try to approach you, to give
You a season of wheat blossoms, dying to tease you
A deep breath in the palm of hand
Like a cat's small mouth singing in reply
Music and poetry, for me to smell
The light and graceful fleeing trace
—— Brimming behind the mountain

117．

牽牛花 陳宗遠

綠蔓如藤不用栽，淡青花繞竹籬開。
披衣向曉還堪愛，忽見蜻蜓帶露來。

The Morning Glory Chen Zongyuan

Green vines creep into an overgrowth
 of tendrils without gardening, some
 tilting at a drunken angle towards

the ground, some groping their blind
　　passage into air; frail flowers, of a
　　　　variety of pale colors, bloom into

trumpets against the bamboo fence,
　　wrapping themselves round it as if
　　　　hanging on for dear life, and giving up
their tendrils to the wind as fluidly as
　　tentacles in water. Loveable is the morning
　　　　glory when the early morning finds me

admiring the flower with my clothes
　　thrown on, which is graced by a dewy
　　　　dragonfly flying and flitting, and alighting.

我瞧見……　　　　　　　　　　　　　林明理

1.
在這海濱草地上，一群潛鳥
唱著我似懂非懂的歌，
即使風在訕笑──我們仍成了知己。

2.
總有一天我會
在你必經的老雲杉上，用野百合的
春歌，同你聊聊天。

3.
我願是紅腹濱鷸，
飛越千里……
只為了相聚時分秒不差。

I Saw⋯⋯

Lin Ming-Li

1.
On the coastal meadow, a flock of diving birds
Are singing songs which I half understand,
Even if the wind is laughing — we have become close friends.

2.
Some day I will
On the old spruce trees by which you are to pass, with the spring songs
Of wild lilies, to have a chat with you.

3.
I wish I were a red knot,
Flying for thousands of miles⋯⋯
Just to be strictly punctual in getting together.

雨後池上

劉攽

一雨池塘水面平，淡磨明鏡照簷楹。
東風忽起垂楊舞，更作荷心萬點聲。

The Pool After the Rain

Liu Ban

A heavy rain fills the pool with
    water to the brim, like a big mirror
        which is gently cleaned, to mirror

the eaves and pillars of the house.
    A sudden gust of east wind blows
        the willow twigs into dancing,

and thousands of raindrops are
    produced to drop on lotus leaves,
        like scattered pearls on the ground.

我不歎息、注視和嚮往 　　　　　林明理

古老的村塘
凝碧在田田的綠荷上
我們曾經雀躍地踏遍它倒影的淺草
看幾隻白鴨
從水面銜起餘光
一個永遠年輕卻不再激越的回音
在所有的漣漪過後　猶響

I Don't Sigh, Look and Long For
Lin Ming-Li

The ancient pond in the village
Heavy green is gathered upon lotus leaves
We have ever walked cheerfully through the weeds of its reflection
To see a few white ducks
Picking up the setting sun from water
An echo forever young yet passionate no more
Still echoing after all ripples have disappeared

119．

題西林壁　　　　　　　　　　　　蘇軾

橫看成嶺側成峰，遠近高低各不同。
不識廬山真面目，只緣身在此山中。

The True Aspect of Lushan Mountain
Su Shi

Viewed horizontally, it is a ridge;
   vertically, a peak. High and low,
     far and near, Lushan Mountain

varies according as the landscape
   is differently clothed — a pregnant
     reflection. Illusory is the true

aspect of the mountain, height
   over height, forest over forest,
     where we find ourselves.

玉山頌[27]　　　　　　　　　　　　林明理

站在雪地上，仰望、傾聽。
我期待你的歌聲，堅毅
深情如母親河。

---

[27] 新聞報導，臺灣最高峰的玉山下了第一場雪，因而為詩。

Ode to Yushan[28]   Lin Ming-Li

Standing on the snowy ground, to looking up, and to listen.
I look forward to hearing your singing, firm
Affectionate like the motherly river.

---

120 •

六月二十七日望湖樓醉書五絕（其一）
蘇軾

黑雲翻墨未遮山，白雨跳珠亂入船。
卷地風來忽吹散，望湖樓下水如天。

Tipsy at Lake-view Pavilion (1)   Su Shi

An endless bed of grey moves over
   the sky and mountain, murky clouds
      churning like Chinese ink, which bring

sheets of rain that smudges the color and
   contours out of everything, yet a distant
      hill has not been completely screened

from view. White raindrops bounce like
   pearls, beating the boat. Gusts of earth-
      rolling wind scatter the clouds, and

---

[28] It is reported in the news that the highest peak of Yushan in Taiwan has its first snowfall, hence the poem.

the water of the West Lake, under the
    pavilion, stills and is one with the sky.

北極燕鷗[29]   林明理

一群群，一對對
在雲層之上
飛過高山和重洋
飛過海灣和激流
——數萬里遠，
為了生存
為了繁殖
努力向前
在南極的浮冰上越冬。
冬去春來
兩極之路，
成為他們共同的方向，
勇者亦如此。

The Arctic Tern[30]   Lin Ming-Li

Flocks after flocks
Above the clouds after clouds
Fly over mountains and oceans

---

[29] 北極燕鷗（The Arctic tern）是候鳥，牠們在北極繁殖，卻要飛到南極去越冬，每年在兩極之間往返一次，行程數萬公里，是世界上飛得最遠的鳥類。

[30] The Arctic tern is a kind of migratory birds which multiply in the Arctic before flying to Antarctica for winter. They migrate back and forth between the two poles annually for thousands of kilometers, for which they are believed to be the birds which travel the longest distance in the world.

Fly over bays and rapids
— Thousands of miles away
To survive
To multiply
Striving forward
To winter on the Antarctic floating ice
Out with winter and in with spring
The road between the two poles
Become their common direction
The same for the brave

121 ·

飲湖上初晴後雨 蘇軾

水光瀲灩晴方好,山色空濛雨亦奇。
欲把西湖比西子,淡妝濃抹總相宜。

The West Lake: Sunny or Rainy Su Shi

Sunny, the waves are dimpling
   in the sunshine, all the air flashes
      and sparkles; rainy, surrounding hills

are hazy and misty — a constantly
   wonderful scene. The West Lake
      can be compared to an ancient beauty,

whose beauty is in the eye of the
   beholder: made-up light or heavy.

金池塘　　　　　　　　　　林明理

風在追問杳然的彩雲
遠近的飛燕在山林的
背影掠過

羞澀的石榴
醉人的囈語，出沒的白鵝
伴著垂柳戲波

秋塘月落
鏡面，掛住的
恰是妳帶雨的明眸

The Golden Pond　　　　　Lin Ming-Li

The wind is chasing after colorful clouds into the distance
The swallows far and near fly
Over the forest in the mountain

The shy pomegranates
Intoxicating words, white geese appearing and disappearing
Frolicking in the waves kissed by weeping willows

The moon falling over the autumn pond
The mirror mirrors
Your bright eyes with rain

122·

海棠 蘇軾

東風嫋嫋泛崇光,香霧空濛月轉廊。
只恐夜深花睡去,故燒高燭照紅妝。

Crabapple Flowers Su Shi

The east wind gently
   blows in spring, as fair
      as crabapple flowers.

Flowery fragrance in
   the fog, the moon is slowly
      moving past the corridor.

Lest the flowers fall asleep
   deep into the night, I hold
      a candle to admire them.

金風鈴 林明理

你是春天的精靈
漫在空氣裡
捎來愉悅的信息
像是突如其來的吻
一隻蝴蝶翩翩而來
你便隨風起舞
我沒有忘記
當年回首的那一刻
你的光芒
穿越黃昏的靜寂

Golden Chimes   Lin Ming-Li

You are the fairy of spring
Dissolving in the air
Bringing pleasant news
Like a sudden surprise kiss
A butterfly is nearing while dancing
And you dance in the wind
I have not forgotten
The moment you glance back that year
Your rays of light
Penetrate the stillness of evening

123 ·

橫塘   范成大

南浦春來綠一川，石橋朱塔兩依然。
年年送客橫塘路，細雨垂楊系畫船。

Hengtang Road   Fan Chengda

With the arrival of spring
  to the riverside south
    of the town, the water

is all rippling with green;
  stone bridges and red
    pagodas still remain. On

宋詩明理搓千載
古今抒情詩三百首
漢英對照

time-honored Hengtang
　Road, I see my friends
　　off, from year to year;

in the drizzling rain, and
　on the green willow tree,
　　a painted boat is tethered.

在思念的角落　　　　　　　　　　　林明理

在想你之前
我是輕吻春風的苦楝花
那深湛的海水
在星宿相繼出現的夜空下
那童真的夢想
是我魂牽夢縈之所在
把我的眸子頃刻點亮

在想你之前
我變成復歸夏雨的燕子
看哪，濁水溪近了
又遠了
那聲音緩緩悠悠
母親的燈
通往我長夜的思量

木麻黃青青
秋風步伐婉轉
母親的微笑
幻成古琴絲弦
把我縈繞其中
每一個回憶都那麼真實
感恩的心似清囀的雲雀

那鬱金色的田野
日夜撩撥我的詩思
火紅的夕陽
重複著故鄉徐緩的音調
而我，無止息的
用筆桿推敲著自己的心
彷若月亮沉入碧潭

在想你之前
我是輕叩秋霜的葉
詩，是繆斯女神的音符
能跨越國界
也能傳承自己的文化
在我想著的時刻
總能占領我的心

在想你之前
我是追逐冬雪的小馬
在思念的角落
故鄉是一支徐緩的長笛
它喚起了我欲飛躍的姿勢
那熟悉的天空
又觸碰了我的夜心

In a Corner of Yearning   Lin Ming-Li

Before thinking of you
I am the neem flower kissing spring wind
The sea water which is deep blue
Under the night sky where stars appear one after another
That innocent dream
Where my heart and soul linger
To forthwith lighten up my eyes

宋詩明理搓千載
古今抒情詩三百首
漢英對照

Before thinking of you
I become a swallow returning into the summer rain
Look, the creek of turbid water is nearing
And far away again
The voice is lingering and melodious
Mother's lamp
Leads to the thoughts of my lengthy night

Green is Casuarina
The autumn wind blows gently
Mother's smile
Fantasized into the chord of an ancient zither
To encircle me
Each memory is so real
A grateful heart is like the sharp-throated skylark

The lushly golden field
Day and night stirs up my poetic thoughts
The fiery setting sun
Repeats the gentle tone of hometown
And I, endlessly
With a pen in my heart
As if the moon has sunk into the blue lake

Before thinking of you
I am the leaf tapping at autumn frost
Poetry is the musical notes of Muse
Which can cross national borders
As well as inheriting one's own culture
While thinking about it
My heart is occupied

Before thinking of you
I am a pony running after winter snow
In a corner of yearning
Hometown is a slow flute

Which awakens my posture of flight
The familiar sky
Once again touches my heart in the night

124．

寄題西湖並送淨慈顯老　　　　　　范成大

南北高峰舊往還，芒鞋踏遍兩山間。
近來卻被官身累，三過西湖不見山。

To the West Lake and the Monk
　　　　　　　　　　　　　Fan Chengda

I used to commute between the
　　South Peak and the North Peak;
　　　　in straw sandals, I have covered

and recovered all the paths between
　　the two peaks. But in recent years
　　　　I have been cumbered with my

official position: for three times I
　　have passed by the West Lake, without
　　　　sparing time to revisit the two peaks.

九份黃昏　　　　　　　　　　　　林明理

初夏蹲踞的霧氣散後
小鎮開始從回憶中醒來

茶樓與紅燈籠高低錯落
古老的礦坑仍殘留著
些許漫長蕭瑟的夢
驀然回首石階前我瞥見
在褪去的灰空下我們曾緩一緩腳步
在落羽的山風與一朵朵傘花中

Dusk in Jiufen Lin Ming-Li

After the sitting fog in early summer disperses
The small town begins to awaken from its memories.
Tea houses and red lanterns are high and low
The old mine is still lingering
Some lengthy and faded dreams
Suddenly glancing back to find before the stone steps
We have ever slowed down our steps under the faded sky
In the mountain wind flying with plumes and many an umbrella flowers

---

125 ·

畫眉鳥 歐陽修

百囀千聲隨意移，山花紅紫樹高低。
始知鎖向金籠聽，不及林間自在啼。

The Blackbird Ouyang Xiu

chirps and twitters as she pleases,
　in the mountain red and purple
　　with flowers: some high, some low.

In the woods, the blackbird
   enjoys more freedom and ease
      than being locked in a golden cage.

棕熊   林明理

空曠溪谷的邊緣
一隻棕熊
閒晃著，吃草
春天，歌聲輕輕掠過
雪、土壤與樹
萬物也融洽於一切靜寂
牠，慢移在岩間
回想起再也無法感受的童年
靜靜等待鮭魚返鄉時
孤獨的影像
彷彿大地的史詩

The Brown Bear   Lin Ming-Li

At the edge of an open valley
A brown bear
Is grazing leisurely
In spring, songs gently pass by
Snow, soil and trees
Myriads of things are harmonious in silence
It moves slowly in the rocks
Recalling its childhood that is no more
Quietly waiting for the return of salmons
The lonely image
Like the epic of the earth

126·

夏日田園雜興十二首（其一）　　　范成大

梅子金黃杏子肥，麥花雪白菜花稀。
日長籬落無人過，惟有蜻蜓蛺蝶飛。

Miscellanies of the Four Seasons (1)
Fan Chengda

Plums golden and apricots
　　plump; buckwheat flowers
　　　　snow-white and rape flowers

sparse. Hedges in the village
　　see lengthening days without
　　　　any passer-by; only dragon-

flies and butterflies are
　　flitting and flying freely.

與主說話　　　林明理

1.
我是一隻旅行的包裹
不知會被帶往何方
但我幾乎可以辨識
絕不會迷失於森林
也不會飛上天空
無論前路有多遠
我都會心存感激

2.
我願
為自己的理念而戰
寬容並善待周遭親友
我願
化成一塊山岩
在柔風親吻大海的時刻
輕輕吟詠祢的聖名

Words With My Lord Lin Ming-Li

1.
I am a traveling package
Without knowing the destination
But I can almost recognize
Never to be lost in the forest
Nor will I fly into the sky
No matter how far the road is
I will remain grateful

2.
I want to
Fight for my own ideals while being
tolerant and kind to my relatives and friends
I want to
Turn into a rock
To whisper your holy name
When the gentle wind is kissing the sea

宋詩明理接千載
古今抒情詩三百首
漢英對照

127·

除夜自石湖歸苕溪（其一）   姜夔

細草穿沙雪半銷，吳宮煙冷水迢迢。
梅花竹裡無人見，一夜吹香過石橋。

Going Home from the Stone Lake On New Year's Eve (1)   Jiang Kui

Tender grass is rooting above
  the sand when the snow has
    half melted; a distant view:

the palace of King Wu looms
  through a cold thin mist over
    the river, which is running

far away. Some plum flowers
  are blossoming in the grove
    of bamboos, to the sight of

nobody, and overnight, the
  scent is wafted, spreading and
    diffusing, across the stone bridge.

長長的思念   林明理

我願是幽谷，
晨露裡的洛神花，
在一條小徑上，
聽紅嘴黑鵯頻頻輕喚……
只要有藍蜻蜓、蝴蝶

快樂地踩著舞步，
白鷺翩飛
在我的臂彎之中。

我願是原野，
在通往兒時的小路，
聽一群小燕子
低聲呢喃……
只要從田埂的邊緣，
聽早起的老農
在我的心上
彼此笑談、問候。

我願是長風，
越過熟悉的溪流，
在返鄉的空中
盡情地奔馳……
只要我思念的人
帶著淺淺的笑容，
我便可以觸及夢裡的
父親　暖暖的手。

Long-lasting Longing   Lin Ming-Li

I wish I were a deep valley,
A roselle flower in the morning dew,
Along a path,
Listen to the constant twitters of red-billed blackbirds....
So long as there are blue dragonflies and butterflies
Dancing joyfully,
White egrets flying
Into my arms.

I wish I were a field,
Along the path leading to my childhood,
Listen to a bevy of swallows
Murmuring softly....
So long as from the edge of the ridge,
Listen to the old farmers who get up early
In my heart
Laughing and greeting each other.

I wish I were the long wind,
Crossing the familiar stream,
In the air of returning home
To run away freely....
So long as the person I pine for
Brings a faint smile,
I can touch Father's warm hands
In my dream.

128 ·

除夜自石湖歸苕溪（其二）　　　姜夔

黃帽傳呼睡不成，投篙細細激流冰。
分明舊泊江南岸，舟尾春風颭客燈。

Going Home from the Stone Lake On New Year's Eve (2)

Jiang Kui

The yellow-capped boatmen
   are talking loudly to each other,
     preventing the sleepy man from

dropping asleep; the boat bamboo
　　into water, to gently touch and
　　　　crack the thin film of ice. My

memory remains fresh: this is
　　the very bank of the Southern
　　　　Shore where we have ever anchored

in some night: spells after spells
　　of spring wind blowing the
　　　　lamp at the stern to be flickering.

春語　　　　　　　　　　　　　　林明理

光暈下
冬不拉[31]的草原
蹄聲和羊群於
牛背托起的太陽

雲霞被召喚
便攜著畫捲兒
嫋嫋到山樹下

在這個瞬間
我把心愛的詩集合上
夜已退隱。而外界
失去雍容、鐘擺和激昂。

只有你，引我思念
如夢的搖藍
綿延在天山

---

[31] 「冬不拉」是一種哈薩克族民間流行的彈撥樂器。

Words of Spring
Lin Ming-Li

Under the halo
The grassland of Dongbula[32]
The sound of hooves and sheep
The sun lifted by the cow's back

The clouds are summoned
And with the painting scroll
They come under the mountain tree

At this moment
I close my favorite poetry collection
The night has retreated. And the outside world
Has lost its grace, bells and passion.

Only you make me pine
The dreamy cradle
Stretching in the Tianshan Mountain

129·

夏日
寇准

離心杳杳思遲遲，深院無人柳自垂。
日暮長廊聞燕語，輕寒微雨麥秋時。

---

[32] "Dongbula" is a popular plucking instrument for the Kazakh people.

The Early Summer
                                   Kou Zhun

The parting sorrows are nowhere
  to be seen, and sluggish is my train
    of thought; deep is the courtyard,

too deep to see a single soul —
  only willows are weeping and
    drooping. At eventide, the swallows

are twittering in the long corridor,
  when the wheat is ripening, after
    a rainfall which brings light cold.

遠方的思念
                                   林明理

我想寄給你，寫在潔淨的
白雲輕靈的翅膀上
在這不是飄雪紛飛的冬天

我想寄給你
豪邁而無形式的歌
以及充滿友情的琴聲

雖然祝福在心中，天涯太遙遠
當你的眼睛逮住這朵雲
你將懂得我唱出的秘密

Longing From Afar
                                   Lin Ming-Li

I want to send it to you, written
On the light wings of white clouds
On the winter day without snow

I want to send it to you
A heroic song without any form
And the sound of zither charged with friendship

With blessing in heart, the horizon too far away
When your eyes catch this blossom of cloud
You will know the secret in my singing

130 ·

淮中晚泊犢頭　　　　　　　　蘇舜欽

春陰垂野草青青，時有幽花一樹明。
晚泊孤舟古祠下，滿川風雨看潮生。

Mooring in the Evening at Riverside Dutou
Su Shunqin

Spring, the overcast sky hanging low;
　　it threatens winds & rains, when bankside
　　　　grass is lushly green; occasionally visible:

a treeful of flowers riotous with various
　　colors in a secluded place, flare to be fair.
　　　　Dusk finds a lonely boat mooring by an

ancient temple, which is watching a river-
　　ful of blowing winds and pelting rains,
　　　　while tide water is rushing and arising.

春雨

林明理

三月的柳
綠
和斜雨
紛揚

三月的塔山
青煙
和暮鴉
飛盪

三月的涼風
偷偷
和雲朵
聚合

雨的冷意
和蹲身的簑影
映射出
春耕的希望

Spring Rain

Lin Ming-Li

The green willows of
March
And the slanting rain
Are swaying

Tashan in March
The blue smoke
And evening crows
Are flying

The cool breeze of March
Stealthily
Gathers with
The clouds

The coldness of the rain
And the shadow of the squatting bamboo
Reflecting
The hope of spring ploughing

---

131 •

鄉思   李覯

人言落日是天涯，望極天涯不見家。
已恨碧山相阻隔，碧山還被暮雲遮。

Homesickness   Li Gou

It is said the spot where the sun
   sets is the horizon; and I look
     longingly beyond the horizon,

still my home is not in view.
   A great pity for me: hills upon
     hills have cut off the connection

between my home and me, and
   the endless hills are veiled
     by boundless murky clouds.

懷鄉　　　　　　　　　　　　　　林明理

在我飄泊不定的生涯裡
曾掀起一個熟悉的聲音
但不久便重歸寂靜

它從何而來？
竟使我深深的足跡追影不及……
游啄的目光分離成渺遠的印記
每一步都是那麼堅定無疑

呵，我心戚戚
那是深夜傳來淒清的弦子
我識得，但如何把窺伺的黎明蒙蔽

Homesickness　　　　　　　Lin Ming-Li

In my wandering life
There has been a familiar voice
Which soon fades into silence

Where did it come from?
It should make my deep footprints fail to catch up……
The wandering sight is separated into remote marks
Each step is so firm and sure

Oh, my heart is sorrowfully laden
Miserable chord through the depth of night
I know, how to veil peeping dawn

132·

碧湘門 陶弼

城中煙樹綠波漫,幾萬樓臺樹影間。
天闊鳥行疑沒草,地卑江勢欲沉山。

The Green City Gate Tao Bi

The city of Changsha is green
  with lush trees, permeating
    like green waves; thousands

of towers and pavilions are
  stowed away in the shade of
    dancing trees. The boundless

sky is punctuated with lines
  of birds, seemingly flying
    into the wild weed; in the low-

lying terrain, the rushing Xiang
  River seems to drown the
    high-rising blue mountain.

白冷圳之戀[33] 林明理

你,是水圳工程的驕傲
新社的母親

---

[33] 白冷圳是台灣台中市一條水圳,因 1999 年 9 月 21 日,台灣歷經大地震,使白冷圳管線受損變形。後來它又被台中縣政府就地重建。它就像是台中新社地區的母親,源源不絕地提供當地的水資源,也是台灣水利工程的驕傲。如今它已成當地人飲水思源的象徵,也成了歷史活教材。

悠揚的山歌
那些輕拂而過的
音和雀鳥在黃昏中回轉
我便翻山越嶺
在風中
尋找你澄碧的眼眸
尋找你熾熱不落的靈魂
及守候老家鄉的靜默

你來自大甲溪，歷經風霜和
那場震變
又重新給人安慰
新社的母親啊
你灌溉了
無數旅人與遊子的心田
如星雨般動容
在群山環抱下
水聲如琴，交錯於
時間之流與月光之中

Love of the Bethlehem Ditch[34]

Lin Ming-Li

You are the pride of the water project
The mother of New Town
The melodious folk songs

---

[34] The Bethlehem Ditch is a water project in Taichung, Taiwan. On September 21, 1999, Taiwan has experienced an earthquake to the damage of the pipeline, which was reconstructed by Taichung County Government. Like the mother of area of Taichung News Agency, it serves as an endless stream of local water resource, and it is also the pride of water conservancy projects in Taiwan. Now it has become a symbol of the source of drinking water for local people, and has become a vivid textbook of history.

The sweeping sound in the wind
And the birds flying through dusk
I climb over the mountains
In the wind
In search of your eyes sparkling with green
Of your warm and unfailing soul
And the silence of guarding hometown

You are from Dajia Stream, through winds & frosts
And the earthquake
And to give people new comfort
O mother of New Town
You have irrigated
The hearts of countless travelers and wanderers
Touching like as the starry rain
Enclosed with mountains
The sound of running water like zither, intermixed
In the stream of time and the moonlight

---

133 ·

西樓 曾鞏

海浪如雲去卻回，北風吹起數聲雷。
朱樓四面鉤疏箔，臥看千山急雨來。

In the West Tower Zeng Gong

Great breakers are like heavy
   clouds, which spread away, and
     roll back; the north wind is on

the blowing, punctuated with
   a few cracking thunders. The
      curtains about the red tower, I

roll them up one by one; then
   I sit idle, to watch thousands of
      mountains caught in a torrential rain.

短詩十帖   林明理

1.
雨林欲哭泣。
比它更驚惶的夜
在赤道徘徊。

2.
夢裡的冰川
留下企鵝的儀隊。
正東瞅西望。

3.
海上的殘雪
喞起暮春的經聲。
雨點敲荷葉。

4.
啊，櫻雪，漫漫，
同鐘塔的月道別。
正像個僧侶。

5.
天鵝的旋舞
柴可夫斯基的夜
在夢中起伏。

宋詩明理接千載
古今抒情詩三百首
漢英對照

6.
雨落柿子樹
水鹿諦聽的湖，像
蕭邦的舞曲。

7.
從林濤中躍出
三月的白色山脈
梅，站成永恆。

8.
蘆花飛白了。
翱翔的天宇間的
鴻雁在唱歌。

9.
夜，墊著腳尖
蠟冬又從雨中來。
聽古寺鐘聲。

10.
詩，在暮鼓裡
山茶，清水竹音的
梵唱中，浮顯。

Ten Short Poems   Lin Ming-Li

1.
The rain forest is on the verge of crying.
It is more startled than the night
Wandering about the equator.

2.
Glaciers in the dream
Leaving behind the penguins' ceremonial procession.
Looking east and west.

3.
The remnant snow at sea
Picking up the sound of scriptures in late spring.
Raindrops beating on lotus leaves.

4.
Ah, boundless snow of cherry blossoms,
Bidding adieu to the moon over the clock tower.
Like a monk.

5.
The spinning dance of swans,
The night of Tchaikovsky
Undulates in the dream.

6.
Rain falls on the persimmon tree
The lake where the deer listen, like
The dance music of Chopin.

7.
Leaping out of forest
The white mountains of March
The plum, standing into eternity.

8.
The reed flowers turn white.
Soaring in the sky
The geese are singing.

9.
The night, on tiptoes;
Winter comes again from the rain.
To listen to the sound bells from the ancient temple.

10.
Poetry, in the evening drum;
Mountain tea, like clear water and bamboo piping
The Buddhist chanting, arising.

---

134 ·

延州 沈括

二郎山下雪紛紛，旋卓穹廬學塞人。
化盡素衣冬不老，石油多似洛陽塵。

The Border Town of Yanzhou   Shen Kuo

Erlang Mountains are are white
  and whiter with snow falling
    and fallen, when yurts are made,

to copy the nomadic life of
  frontier people. Petroleum as
    the burner, when winter is still

young, my plain clothes are plain
  no more: soiled with smoke,
    like rolling dust in the capital city.

冬之雪　　　　　　　　　　　　　　　　林明理

說起北方
到底有多遠
讓你忍不住流下淚
回鄉路太長
只得把它折疊入夢
啊母親的手
從荊棘叢中向我伸來
撫摸著我苦楚的童年

Winter Snow　　　　　　　　　　　Lin Ming-Li

Concerning the north
How far is it
It brings tears out of your eyes
The homeward road is too long
Which cannot but be folded into my dream
Oh Mother's hands
Reach out to me from the thorny thicket
To fondle my painful childhood

曉霽　　　　　　　　　　　　　　　　司馬光

夢覺繁聲絕，林光透隙來。
開門驚鳥鳥，餘滴落蒼苔。

宋詩明理接千載
古今抒情詩三百首
漢英對照

A Fine Morning After the Night Rain
Sima Guang

Waking up from a nightlong
   sound sleep, I find thickly
      falling rain let up; wisps

and beams of morning sun-
   shine reach me after penetrating
      forest leaves. Upon my

pushing open the door, crows
   and magpies are startled into
      a hurried flight, who shake
down from their branches
   drops of water on the green
      moss, splashing and spattering.

拂曉之前
林明理

沒一點雜色
林中
點點水光忽隱忽顯

郁郁杜松
孕出螞蟻的卵
隨荊棘聲愜意地伸長

一叢野當歸縮在樹牆旁幽坐
像是沉醉於
命運的遐想

Before Dawn   Lin Ming-Li

No mottled color
In the forest
Dots of watery light flicker

Lush junipers
Gestating with the eggs of ants
Stretching out leisurely with the sound of thorns

A cluster of wild Chinese angelica huddles to sit quietly
beside the wall of trees
As if intoxicated
In the reverie of fate

---

136 ·

夢   呂本中

夢入長安道，萋萋盡春草。
覺來春已去，一片池塘好。

A Dream   Lü Benzhong

In a dream I come to
　a broad way of Chang'an,
　　the capital, where grass

grows green here and there,
　without a single soul.
　　Awake, I find spring

gone, when the pool
   presents itself before
      my eyes, fair and square.

星夜 林明理

這麼多
流星雨

掠過古老山脈
雪花般
晶亮

沒人曉得
它跋涉的路徑
只有透露的風聲

讓我
浮想聯翩

The Starry Night Lin Ming-Li

So many
Meteor showers

Passing over age-old mountains
Like snowflakes
Brilliantly bright

Nobody knows
Its road of trekking
Only the revealing wind

Gives rein to
My imagination

137・

慶全庵桃花　　　　　　　　　　　　謝枋得

尋得桃源好避秦，桃紅又是一年春。
花飛莫遣隨流水，怕有漁郎來問津。

Peach Flowers at a Small Buddhist Temple　　　Xie Fangde

The Land of Peach Blossoms
   is an ideal place to evade the
     chaos caused by war; with red

peach flowers another spring
   is in flight. Please do not let
     fallen peach flowers flow

with the running creek, lest
   fishermen trace back to this
     secluded land of milk and honey.

黑夜無法將你的光和美拭去　　　　　林明理

當地平線第一道黎明
向沉睡中的你歌唱
牧場在潺潺小溪的霧雲下甦醒
所有的眼睛都注視著
你，活著的意志，眉宇的神情
已不再遲鈍沉悶
你像遠空之鷹

在翠嶺間自由穿行
聽萬木的呼吸,雛鳥的輕啼
那蜜蜂,正採擷清甜的汁液

縱然剎那,就讓宙斯尋思
為你而閃明,在綠蔭的沉默裡
旋律從我心底響起,在你遠離之際
黑夜無法將你的光和美拭去
噢,如果眾人之主聽得見
我真切地祝禱,而地域也不再有距離
就讓這峽谷捲起回音吧
細弱的和風已頻頻翹首
在這條石徑上緩行
萬木跟著你的腳步而揮手
你篇章的詩情
確已創造了人間的泉源,萬古常青

The Dark Night Fails to Wipe Out Your Beauty and Light   Lin Ming-Li

When the first dawning light in the horizon
Sings to you who are sound asleep
The pasture wakes up under the clouds over the babbling creek
All the eyes are attentive
On you, the living will, the expression in the eyes
No more drowsy and sluggish
You are like an eagle in the boundless sky
Freely flying among emerald mountains
Listen to the breath of myriads of trees, the gentle chirping of young birds
The bees are gathering sweet juice

In an instant, for Zeus to meditate
To flash for you, in the silence of the green shade
The melody is arising from the bottom of my heart, upon your leaving afar
The dark night fails to wipe out your beauty and light
Oh, if the leader of the crowd can hear it
Honestly I pray, and there is no distance between regions
Let the valley be aloud with echoes
The gentle breeze is on the stirring
Slowly creeping along the stony path
Myriads of trees follow your steps while waving hands
The poetry of your pieces
Has really created a fountain in the world, forever green

138 ·

春晴　　　　　　　　　　　　　　　　　王安石

新春十日雨，雨晴門始開。
靜看蒼苔紋，欲上人衣來。

A Fine Spring Day　　　　　　　Wang Anshi

New spring witnesses a rain-
    fall through ten days;
        the door is not open until

it lets up. In quietude I watch
    the green growing moss,
        feeling it invading my clothes.

愛在德爾斐[35]   林明理

蜿蜒的河流,獨留蒼鷹
不斷地重述德爾斐的憂鬱。
牠的歌聲中,鋪敘
許多古老的傳說。那是自由的音律,
比風笛還悠揚,
比詩還奇麗。
牠凌駕於山海與古城,
擁抱無垠的宇宙——
只為一個愛的許諾,翱翔於蒼穹。

Love at Delphi[36]   Lin Ming-Li

Meandering river, goshawks are left alone,
Delphic melancholy is restated time and again.
His singing is interlarded with
A lot of ancient legends. That is free melody
Which is more melodious than the bagpipe,
More wonderful than a poem.
Lording it over the mountain-sea and the ancient city,
It embraces the boundless universe —
Just for the promise of love, soaring in the sky.

---

[35] 傳說希臘宙斯曾經於相反方向放出兩隻蒼鷹來測量大地,而它們相遇的地點正是古代希臘的聖地德爾斐 Delphi。

[36] Note: Legend has it that the Greek Zeus once sent two goshawks in opposite directions to measure the earth, and the place where they met was Delphi, a holy place in ancient Greece.

139 •

曉行   孔平仲

枕上杜鵑啼，匆匆早起時。
出行天未曉，月在杏花枝。

A Morning Tour   Kong Pingzhong

Cuckoos' twitters
   travel to my pillow
      — time to rise early.

A tour before day-
   break, when a moon
      is effectual through

branches and twigs
   of apricot flowers.

科隆大教堂[37]   林明理

多美的哥德式教堂！
從東岸眺望——
上方，尖塔、星辰、灰藍
下方，河身、橋影、晃蕩
數百年過去了
它仍是西方重要的祭壇
沉睡在星空的樂曲上

---

[37] 在德國萊茵河畔的科隆大教堂 Cologne Cathedral 是世界第三高的教堂，也是世界第三大哥德式教堂，被列名為「世界文化遺產」之一。

Cologne Cathedral[38]   Lin Ming-Li

How spectacular is the Gothic church!
    To gaze from the east coast —
Above, steeple, stars, and gray blue
Below, the river's body, bridge's shadow, waving
Hundreds of years have passed
It is still an important altar in the West
    Slumbering in the starry music

---

140 ·

樓櫸暮歸書所見二首（其二）   唐庚

春著湖煙膩，晴搖野水光。
草青仍過雨，山紫更斜陽。

Evening Return into the Zen Mountain (2)   Tang Geng

Spring is here, and the lake
    is misty with heavy fog;
        under brilliance of the sun,

running water in the field
    is bright with glittering and
        twinkling beams. Washed

---

[38] Cologne Cathedral, by the Rhine River of Germany, is the third tallest church, and the third biggest Gothic church in the world, for which it is listed as one of the "world cultural heritages".

by spring rain, green grass
　is greener, dripping with green;
　　caught in the slanting sun,
　　　the mountain is all crimson.

頌長城　　　　　　　　　　　　　　林明理

春風
給長城帶來幽雅的涼意
它慢慢甦醒在暮色裡
那張輝煌的臉
撩起無數詩人的鄉愁

我夢見自己
輕輕觸及它剛毅的輪廓
如此自然
握暖了我的雙手
彷彿沉浸在莊嚴的芬芳裡

年年歲歲
它驕傲地立在沙丘之緣上
不朽的眼眸
深邃如夜空般的黑藍
無視大漠孤煙的寂寥

朝朝暮暮
它用絕世美麗的歌聲
激勵我奮勇前進
似彩虹鳥向四個方向飛去
只在夢裡才分外清晰

隨它飛吧！
飛入這長空澄碧

我在海峽和波浪間巡行
心繫北國，萬里雪飄
靈魂是一座孤獨的島嶼

Ode to the Great Wall   Lin Ming-Li

The spring breeze
Brings a graceful coolness to the Great Wall
It slowly awakens in the twilight
Its brilliant face
Stirs up the nostalgia of countless poets

I dream of myself
Gently touching its stubborn outline
So naturally
To warm my hands
As if immersed in its solemn fragrance

Year after year
It proudly stands on the edge of the sand dunes
Its immortal eyes
Profound as the dark blue of the night sky
To ignore the solitary column of smoke over the vast desert

Day and night
With its beautiful singing matchless in the world
It inspires me to move forward
Like rainbow birds flying away in four directions
To be clear and distinct in dreams

Fly away with it!
Into the boundless blue sky
I cruise between the waves and the straits
My heart yearns northward, snow flying through thousands of miles
The soul is a solitary island

141 ·

明月溪　　　　　　　　　　　　　　滿執中

月出溪水清，月落溪水黑。
茫茫溪上人，笑與月為客。

Moonlit Creek　　　　　　　　　Man Zhizhong

Moonrise, creek water
　is clear; moonset, creek
　　water is dark. Dim forms

of people by the creek,
　laughingly with the moon
　　as a genial companion.

塞哥維亞舊城[39]　　　　　　　　　林明理

一座孤獨的城堡
　　恰似
　　　　隨風盪漾的船
　　靜靜睡在山崖上
只在夢中，回到中世紀的向晚
雲不曾改變過什麼
　　　群聚的星辰仍宴飲著
　　這一季迷人的月色

---

[39] 西班牙的塞哥維亞（Segovia）舊城，雄踞在一個狹長的山岩上，被列為世界文化遺產。

The Old Town of Segovia[40]   Lin Ming-Li

A lonely castle
   Is like
      A boat waving in the wind
    Sleeping quietly on the cliff
Only in a dream, it returns to the medieval evening
Nothing changed for the clouds
   The gathering stars are still feasting
On the charming moonlight of the season

---

142 ·

書壽昌驛   程俱

歲暮白日速，風高黃葉稀。
歸心與寒雁，一夜向南飛。

An Autumn Scene   Cheng Ju

At the end of the year the day
   quickens its steps; in high wind,
      yellow leaves are flitting and flying.

A cold wild goose and my homeward thoughts are flying south-
      ward through darkness of the night.

---

[40] The old town of Segovia in Spain is located in a long and narrow rock, and is nd is listed as a world cultural heritage.

黑面琵鷺[41]   林明理

來自北國的
  黑面舞者
輕輕掠過
    福爾摩沙
安靜的海岸
或在七股灘地上佇立翻飛
    或在魚塭中覓食
閃光的身影
    仿若唱歌的天使

Black-faced Spoonbill[42]   Lin Ming-Li

Black-faced dancers
  From the north
Gently flies past
    The quiet beach
Of Formosa
Some standing or flying on the Seven-stranded Beach
    Some searching for food in fish ponds
Their flashing forms
    Like the singing angels

---

[41] 全世界黑面琵鷺（Black-faced spoonbill）僅剩不到三千隻，每年來臺灣過冬的黑面琵鷺約有一千多隻。

[42] There are less than three thousand black-faced spoonbills all over the world, and about one thousand migrate to Taiwan each winter.

143 ·

新泉　　　　　　　　　　　　　　　黃庭堅

牆根新冽寒泉眼，風廊一股來冷冷。
燈花夜半知我喜，恰是舊山穿石聲。

A New Mouth of Spring　　　　Huang Tingjian

Beneath the wall there is
　a mouth of spring which
　　is clean and clear; a spell

of wind through the corridor
　blows cold. The midnight
　　wick is privy to my inner

joy, when the old mountain
　is alive with the sound of
　　something through the rock.

濁水溪星夜　　　　　　　　　　　林明理

遠遠天邊，落霞吻孤鶩，
芒花的合唱，
讓我停步……
西螺大橋，秋水共長，
還有斜陽，彎彎的溪畔。

那就是我回眸的——
熟悉的身影呀，

我的故鄉，
紅橋浮在玫瑰天穹，
寧謐的原野，繁星滿河。

驀然，我站在島嶼一隅，
大地仍是睡意綿長，
而我聽到了遠方的呼喚，
像是你悄然出現又像是
童年的時光，靜靜滑翔。

A Starry Night at Zhuoshui Stream
           Lin Ming-Li

In the remote horizon, the setting sun is kissing wild ducks,
The chorus of miso flowers,
Slow and stop my steps....
Xiluo Bridge which nurses the autumn water,
As well as the setting sun, the winding creek.

That is what I look back on —
The familiar form,
My hometown,
The red bridge floating in the rosy sky,
The quiet wilderness, a riverful of stars.

Suddenly, I stand at a corner of the island,
The great earth is still asleep,
And I hear the call from afar,
As if you appear silently, again
Like childhood, on the quiet gliding.

144·

春草   劉敞

春草綿綿不可名，水邊原上亂抽莖。
似嫌車馬繁華地，才入城門便不生。

Spring Grass   Liu Chang

Spring grass grows fair
    and lush, defying description;

by water or in the field,
    it is budding and sprouting.

Seemingly it hates the area
    busy with heavy traffic:

approaching the city gate,
    it diminishes, tapering off……

愛的讚頌   林明理

愛情是不敗的經典老歌，
它歌詠人間的悲歡，
就算會無所適從，
還是想架勢十足地放手一搏。

總想一起談心，在花間月下，
總想完成閃現的夢想，
保持堅強，絕不退縮，
不讓愛情褪色。

當它深邃的眼瞳
喚醒你內在的力量，
你將會明白——
比起愛情，天國已不算什麼。

In Praise of Love   Lin Mingli

Love is an unbeatable classic song,
Which eulogizes worldly joys and sorrows,
Even if at a loss,
Still a try with all the might.

A constant wish to talk to each other, among moonlit flowers,
A constant wish to fulfill the flashing dream,
Stay strong, never to cringe and cower,
Not for love to fade and fail.

When its deep pupils
Awaken your inner strength,
You will understand —
Compared to love, heaven is n

晚春途中   張公庠

一年春事已成空，擁鼻微吟半醉中。
夾路桃花風雨過，馬蹄無處避殘紅。

宋詩明理接千載
古今抒情詩三百首
漢英對照

En Ruote in Late Spring   Zhang Gongxiang

The test-takers who failed
　　in the annual imperial spring
　　　　test are riding horses back;

crestfallen, they seem to be
　　half drunk; spring things,
　　　　all in vain. Peach flowers,

blown and beaten by the rain,
　　fall aground in profusion,

the horse hooves fail to
　　shun stamping on them.

在愛情來臨之前   林明理

在愛情來臨之前，
我要以每秒千里的速度，
飛往那一天。我謳歌相遇，
為了這一刻，我想飛，
看看天空上到底刻了些什麼詩句。

在愛情來臨之前，
我不可以只做夢，忘了閱讀
它的詩篇。它永遠不會變，
只有戀人改變它的樣貌，
讓愛佈滿荊棘，更顯得明顯。

啊，誰能預知它的開端和結尾？
誰能抗拒它美麗的輪廓？
讓它佔據心靈的首席？

在愛情來臨之前，
我將側耳傾聽它崇高的秘密。

在愛情來臨之前，
我不知它將來自何方？
只把它藏進我的臂彎，
儘管它仍是無可救藥，
我依然想對它說，慶幸有你。

Before the Advent of Love   Lin Ming-Li

Before the advent of love,
I want to fly to that day with a speed
Of a thousand miles per second. I eulogize the encounter;
For this moment, I want to fly,
To see what poetic lines are engraved in the sky.

Before the advent of love,
I cannot just dream, and forget to read
Its poems. It will never change,
Only lovers can change its appearance,
For love to be filled with thorns, more obvious.

Ah, who can predict its beginning and end?
Who can resist its beautiful silhouette?
Who lets it occupy the first place in the soul?
Before the advent of love,
I will be all ears to its sublime secrets.

Before the advent of love,
I do not know where will it come?
I only hide it in my arms,
Though it is still incurable,
And I want to say to it: lucky to be with you.

146·

雙燕　　　　　　　　　　　　　　　　　　范成大

底處飛雙燕，銜泥上藥欄。
莫教驚得去，留取隔簾看。

Twin Swallows　　　　　　　　　　　Fan Chengda

Twin swallows, from nowhere,
　are alighting on the balustrade
　　with mud in their beaks. Take

care: not to startle them away —
　it's advisable to peep at them
　　stealthily through the curtain.

曾經　　　　　　　　　　　　　　　　　　林明理

沿著古老橋畔，落日懸在綠野，
你的沉默隨著芒草花變得苦澀，
然後秋菊睡著了，村野的兩旁，
稻浪也不再搖曳；
那潛藏的秘密，羞紅著臉的熱火
將回你以無人知道的憂傷。

只有風兒藏進我的衣袖，
轉眼，又在大片花海上消匿。
沿著地球邊界，水聲鬱鬱，
我的摯友，你可好？

離別太匆匆⋯⋯恰如山谷百合，
收攏起我思念的故鄉。

Once Lin Mingli

Along the ancient bridge, the setting sun hangs over green field;
Your silence turns bitter with grass flowers;
Then autumn chrysanthemums fall asleep, to both sides of the village;
The rice waves sway no more.
The hidden secret, the blushing heat
Will return you with unknown sorrow.

Only wind hides itself in my sleeves;
In the blink of an eye, it disappears again into a sea of flowers.
Along the border of the earth, doleful sound of water,
My dear friend, how are you?
The farewell is in such a hurry.... like the lilies in the valley,
To collect the hometown for which I pine.

147·

夜雨 呂本中

夢短添惆悵，更深轉寂寥。
如何今夜雨，只是滴芭蕉？

The Night Rain

Lü Benzhong

A short dream redoubles
   the sorrow; the depth of night
      adds to loneliness. Why

the raindrops tonight are
   constantly dropping on and
      dripping in the banana leaves?

短詩一束

林明理

1.
紅瓦屋,蟬鳴的院子。
驕陽橫在故里。

2.
草聲斷虹彩,
一閃一滅深澗上,
寂寞翩翩叩響。

3.
大王蓮啊,
橫推水波,昂首爭雄。

4.
落霞醉古松,
誦聲拂泉湧。

5.
月桃花,綴滿山野,
雲豹藏進煙霧。

6.
孤鷺返水鄉,
邊看溪橋,邊朝田野飛去,
原是故鄉路。

7.
妳的微笑,
宛若拂草的蝴蝶,
引我諦聽風中醉語。

A Bunch of Short Poems   Lin Ming-Li

1.
A red-tiled house with courtyard full of cicadas.
The sun is shining in my hometown.

2.
The sound of grass cuts off the rainbow,
It flickers and fades in the deep creek,
Loneliness knocking and resounding.

3.
Oh, great lotus,
To push the water waves, holding head high to compete for supremacy.

4.
The setting sun intoxicated in ancient pines,
The fountain sound brushes the spring.

5.
The moon-peach flowers, filling the fields and mountains,
The clouded leopards hide themselves in the fog.

6.
The lone heron returns to the land of water,
Looking at the bridge over a stream, it flies into fields,
It turns out to be the road to my hometown.

7.
Your smile,
Like a butterfly fondling the grass,
It allures me to listen to the drunken words in the wind.

148 ·

江上 俞桂

小雨才收日漸斜，酒旗插處兩三家。
江頭妝點秋來景，半是蘆花半蓼花。

On the River   Yu Gui

A slight rain slowly slows
   down to naught when the
      sun is slanting westward;

wine banners are suggestive
   of two or three wine shops.
      The head of the river is

adorned with autumn scene:
   half reed catkins, and
      half smartweed flowers.

你一直在我身邊　　　　　　　　林明理

風雨過後
星星一樣璀璨明淨
飛吧，思念
在那兒——
在冬天的一個晚上

彷彿從地平線的彼岸
傳來了熟悉的聲響
那橫渡的月光啊
將不是虛幻
是我靜默的遐想

你一直在那兒
在薄雪紛飛的
爐火旁
帶著我從未看過的
如清水般的目光

啊，我的朋友
像傳說中的神話
像風帆高掛的大船
轉眼便到眼前……
史詩般的圖像

You are always by my side　　　Lin Ming-Li

After the storm
My yearning
bright as a star
flies toward
a winter night

Where you pace
around a fire
under the flying snow
Your eyes clear
as pure water

Ah, my friend
like a sailing ship
an epic image
a myth of legend
You appear in the blink of an eye……

149 •

松雪　　　　　　　　　　　　　　嚴粲

陰崖未知晴，松雪自在白。
可恨晚風顛，飛寒亂苔石。

Snow on Pine Trees　　　　　Yan Chan

The shaded cliff knows
   no fine days; the snow
      on pine trees are white

by itself. Hateable is
   the evening gale: with
      flying coldness it crazily

overthrows and upturns
   mossy rocks.

短詩五首   林明理

1.
火山灰燼下，老城沉睡了，
時間凝結於千年。

2.
沙諾河畔，水聲嗚咽，
天鵝在徘徊。

3.
未曾來過羅馬，
龐貝已隱沒，只有時間膠囊
慢慢地打開老城的故事。

4.
在赫庫蘭尼姆小鎮中，
那些被埋在浮石之下的
船屋和紙莎草，都在夢中。
天地間一片寧靜！

5.
面對前七世紀建立的輝煌之城
想像
穿越春夜波光流蕩的運河

Five Short Poems   Lin Ming-Li

1.
Under volcano ashes, the old town is sound asleep,
Time is frozen in thousands of years.

2.
By the Sano River, water is wailing;
Swans are strolling.

3.
Not have been to Rome,
Pompeii is buried deep; only a time capsule remains
Slowly to unfold the story of the old city.

4.
In the little town of Herculaneum,
What are buried under pumice
Are houseboats and papyrus, all in a dream.
Perfect peace reigns between heaven and earth!

5.
Facing the glorious city founded in the 7th century BC
To imagine
The brilliant canal flowing through the spring night

---

150 ·

雪夜   趙葵

酒力欺寒淺，心清睡較遲。
梅花擎雪影，和月度疏籬。

A Snowy Night   Zhao Kui

The force of liquor fails
   to keep out the cold; a
      limpid mind guarantees

staying up late into the
   night. Plum blossoms
      hold up the form of snow,

which are reflected, in
   bright moonlight, onto
      the sparse wattled wall.

光點 林明理

冬日一個傍晚,亮得
像銀白鱗片的路;
知更鳥,甜美且有力地,
在林頂上低飛,
又對我繞著圈——就這樣
停在湖面,啄星之影。

啊!有多少個冰晨,又刺穿
多少次樹林懸垂的臉?
每根細枝,每一隻蟲動
在互訴心事,在悸動裏
模糊,是冰已龜裂?
寒裡雪融聲漸濃,又漸遠……

像無數微醺的落葉
我在空氣裡喃喃
這或許,是必然,
也是偶然——
天已暗,松鼠的吱叫
與唯一的想望永訣。

Dots of Light   Lin Ming-Li

A winter evening, a road which
Is bright like silvery scales;
The robin, sweetly and forcefully,
Is flying low over the woods,
While circling above me — thus
Stopping on the lake surface, to peck at the reflected stars.

Ah! How many icy mornings have pierced
The hanging face of the woods? How many times?
Each twig, each squirmy worm
Are pouring out what is on their mind, in the commotion
To be dim, is the ice cracking?
In cold air the sound of melting snow becomes louder,
tapering off….

Like numberless tipsy falling leaves,
I murmur in the air:
Perhaps this is a must-be,
And a might-be —
The sky is dim and dark, the squirrels' squeaking,
To say forever goodbye to the only wish.

附錄：Comments on Tsai, Huei-Cheng's *Studies Of The Novels By Lu Xun*

作　者：蔡輝振
出版者：高雄復文圖書出版社
出版日：2001.09
ISBN 957-555-556-2 平裝

Abstract

Studies of the Novels by Lu Xun is Tsai, Huei-Cheng's lifelong undertaking. He analyzes the actual accomplishments and critical points of Lu Xun's novels from five areas: his creative backgrounds, classification of his works, his writing techniques, exploration of his thoughts, and the status of his styles. It is worthy of further investigation.

Keywords: Lu Xun, novels, aesthetical thoughts.

評蔡輝振的《魯迅小說研究》

臺灣 林明理

摘要

《魯迅小說研究》係蔡輝振一生力作,他從〈創作背景〉、〈作品分類〉、〈寫作技巧〉、〈思想探討〉、〈風格地位〉五範疇,探討魯迅小說的實際成就與評點,值得研究。

關鍵詞:魯迅、小說、美學思想。

一、其人其書

蔡輝振〈1955-〉是個特別的人,他出生於彰化縣臨海僻鄉的小村,個性樸實剛毅;自幼窮困,堅忍苦讀,奮鬥歷程,幾多浮沉,十分令人感動。他有情而且創意十足,曾是兼具理性、感性和知性的成功企業家,但最後公司被倒債而拖垮。他毅然選擇棄商從文,再度拾起書本攻讀,42歲畢業於香港珠海大學文學博士,目前是臺灣省雲林科技大學教授。26至28歲之間,連續三年參加德國、美國及瑞士國際發明展,獲金牌獎等多項殊榮。學術專長於創意研發、文獻數位典藏科際整合、台灣文學、魯迅研究等;並成立「魯迅數位博物館」資料庫、「麗文線上教學」數位學習平台,勤於教學與專案研究。

《魯迅小說研究》是蔡輝振的博士論文,高雄復文出版;內容充實,很重視文獻資料整理的精華點。文筆自然流暢,能準確的提綱挈領,有著他自己實事求是的科學態度。他親自走訪中國多地,也介紹了很多不同學家的評點。這些都啟發於蔡輝振他個人的智慧才華、毅力和學派的觀念及感覺上的優劣。他在第七章總結裡,歸納出魯迅具有"沉鬱、冷峻又執著偏激"的性格,以致於使他在小說作品上,所表現的便是"憂憤沉郁、幽默精煉",呈現著他"冷雋尖刻"的藝術風格。在評論裡作者也提到,他認為魯迅只不過是個社會病理學家,而非社會病療學家。最後,作者研究發現,魯迅及其作品確實很富感染力與煽動力,尤其對於血氣方剛的年輕人更是易受其影響的。作者引用當年名作家蘇雪林、夏志清及梁實秋等對魯迅的批判之詞後,他在建議中提出,大陸今後對魯迅研究方向的修正觀點及對魯迅小說應還以純粹的文學風貌、勿泛政治化的期許。細讀全書,俯仰之間,皆成心得。顯然地,蔡輝振的努力和才情,已經得到了豐富的收穫。

然而,筆者以為,魯迅在歷史上的成就,後代越是遮掩,越是明亮,正像彎月因蒙上黑紗而倍感動人;因為魯迅寫作的熱情曾戰勝艱辛的歲月,在中國兵荒馬亂的苦味中間,魯迅小說的出現才得以呈現無限甘甜。魯迅小說,雖非全然的科學真理,不必過度的迷戀崇拜;但它也不是純粹的偏激,可以被簡單地否定。唯從美學思想上講,魯迅小說確有值得借鏡和學習之處。因此,筆者僅就文本的內容見解,加以分析評述。

二、魯迅小說研究的實質和特點

魯迅〈1881-1936〉原名周樟壽,1898年改為周樹人,是中國重要文學家、思想家、評論家。生於清光緒七年,浙江省

宋詩明理接千載
古今抒情詩三百首 漢英對照

紹興市的一個書香門弟。祖父曾在北京任官員，父親是名秀才。12歲時，祖父因科舉舞弊案而被革職下獄，魯迅兄弟隨即離城被安插到大舅父家中避難；自此，家道衰落，但童年的境遇、紹興十七年的生活場景，也造就了魯迅日後完成的小說《吶喊》、《彷徨》和散文集《朝花夕拾》的思想靈泉。之後，魯迅入南京四年，20歲畢業於南京的礦路鐵路學堂，翌年赴日本七年，入仙台醫學專門學校，學習現代醫學。一年後，因觀看日俄戰爭紀錄片，深感於要救國救民，需先救思想。遂而棄醫從文，他希望用文學改造中國人的"國民劣根性"。這些在作者的第二章裡更有細膩的詳述。

尤令我注目的是，魯迅19-20歲之間，在南京求學階段寫下的詩歌，其中，〈別諸弟三首〉之三：「從來一別又經年，萬里長風送客船。我有一言應記取，文章得失不由天」這是首思鄉情切、寄語其弟周作人寫作上的叮嚀與期勉。而〈蓮蓬人〉是首深刻的美學詩作：「芰裳荇帶處仙鄉，風定猶聞碧玉香。鷺影不來秋瑟瑟，葦花伴宿露瀼瀼。掃除膩粉呈風骨，褪卻紅衣學淡妝。好向濂溪稱淨植，莫隨殘葉墮寒塘。」這首詩確實有自己的內在邏輯，藉蓮來呈現自己，而不失其藝術之為藝術的本質。從這個角度來看，魯迅在20歲時，其美學思想即涵蓋東西文化的洗禮，已能創造出很耐人尋味的詩美境界。魯迅是宋代的周敦頤〈字濂溪〉的後裔子孫，原詩的核心思想是：文學是活的，有生成變化，就如同濂溪先生的獨愛蓮之出淤泥而不染，此詩主題不同於周敦頤細膩的寫實表現，而在流露出賞蓮的自己，也有恬靜的生命力。

而魯迅22歲時在日本留學時寫下的另一首〈自題小像〉詩：「靈臺無計逃神矢，風雨如磐暗故園。寄意寒星荃不察，我以我血薦軒轅。」詩裡滿是張力、悲憤的動勢，其背後隱藏的訊息，明言之，是魯迅對於中國抗戰的記憶映像的綜合呈現與憂思性格的舖現。其中就有魯迅生命的動態和歷史的向度,更賦予古典美學的特性。然而,魯迅總是能多元思想,超越羈絆,而這也是他備受尊崇,不被歷史遺忘的原因。

魯迅歸國後,自創作文學起,直到 55 歲因肺結核和肺氣腫誘發的嚴重氣胸而病世。一生的作品在未來探討魯迅研究上,有不可替代的歷史價值。蔡振輝對魯迅小說的專注、投入、鍥而不捨的收集、整理,是基於對研究主體的觀察入微與真知遠見。他認為,魯迅較擅長於現代白話文的短篇作品,尤其是以諷刺、鄉土小說為主。他雖同意魯迅是國際名作家、文學家,更是新文學運動以來中國最偉大的文藝創作家;但就作品單篇而言,魯迅並非每篇都是傑作。但我隨著研究的深入,反芻在魯迅小說的領域裡,跳脫學派的推崇或輕蔑,留下理性嚴謹深思後的是什麼…?筆者認為只有回歸美學思想(Esthetics thought)才能還原其傑作生命力。

魯迅誕生於中國內憂外患之際,對國力衰微有更直接的切膚之痛,其憤世嫉俗的激情,盡傾注於文學創作之中。他自幼喜好書畫,愛好文藝的傾向源自於其與生俱來的美學思想,既存中國古典文學形跡,又具西方美學風範,深受俄國的果戈理、波蘭的顯克微支以及日本的夏日漱石、森鷗外…等外國文學的影響。故他的小說,決然不會趨時媚俗,而是一種獨闢蹊徑、帶有很強化浪漫愛國思想的主觀相契合。他運用人對事物的美的認識能力和審美評價能力的凝聚,融入了自己的思想感情和審美偏好,從而體現了對揭開舊社會的黑暗的審美理想和抨擊舊思想的腐朽的審美氣質,自創"言簡義重"的新奇風格。魯迅的美學思想主要表現在他擅長的小說中,其特點概括起來有以下兩方面:

1. 人物鮮明 寓意深刻

德國古典美學家康德(Immanuel Kant, 1724-1804)認為,審美判斷不是一種知識,不是一種認知活動,而是一種感覺。而魯迅小說裡的人物塑造,有通俗性及常為悲劇性情節的內容;在很大程度上體現了他天性哲學、破除迷信的宗教理念及文藝思想體系的有機成分。如果說盧梭是法國啟蒙哲學的最主要代表之一,是法國大革命的精神導師;那麼,魯迅他便是愛國主義的崇拜者,他也同樣是中國近代文藝美學的奠基者。

比如《彷徨·在酒樓上》介紹主角"呂緯甫"的描繪:「…細看他相貌,也還是亂蓬蓬的鬚髮;蒼白的長方臉,然而衰瘦了。精神很沉靜,或者卻是頹唐;又濃又黑的眉毛底下的眼睛也失了精采。」這段裡,開啟了中國小說用白話書寫的藝術表現;字的生命可比之於魯迅的精神;他的美學思索並不是純粹的當下,隨即揭示歷史的變動與文化的傷痕。

捷克漢學家雅羅斯拉夫·普實克〈Prusek,Jaroslav〉曾說過,魯迅的興趣顯然不在於創造所能刺激讀者幻想的激動人心的情節,而在別處。這感觸也反映出,魯迅的小說是有目的性的自由創造活動的藝術,且不受制於傳統。他跳脫鏡花水月般的浪漫〈如《紅樓夢》〉,也不取材於幻想〈如《西遊記》或傳奇〈李娃傳〉等通俗體材;反而專以社會基層的平凡小人物為主,用心描繪出當下生活經驗的反照,藉以喚起人們對意蘊空間的想像及對美感的社會性的重視。另外,〈頭髮的故事〉、〈示眾〉等等膾炙人口的小說,作品也具有真實度與想像的拓展,能刻劃多重人物的性格,時而溫馨與詼諧、時而帶有童稚般的熱情、時而感人熱淚;能拉進與讀者間的距離,隱約表露出魯迅的熱血與創作中最平常的快樂。

2. 布局連綿 鄉土意趣

其實，魯迅是很重視小說的節奏和意趣的，在動人的意象及融匯鄉土語言的表達上，也獨具匠心。如《吶喊·故鄉》裡〈故鄉〉的開頭：「我冒著嚴寒，回到相隔二千餘里，別了二十餘年的故鄉。→現在」，與一般散文家散發出的激盪難平情愫有所不同，他把這種鄉土意趣當是他歸國創作心境趨於平靜後的一種反映。作品中經由布局的細膩處理，產生了一種新的建築美學風格。文字精簡，排列創新，→語言符號可以變成包含許多詮釋的模子，也可以將空間與時間延伸化，賦予該內容新鮮的聯想；它更需要讀者的聽、視、觸的多種感覺之投入參與。

如魯迅筆下寫的紹興風情中，有篇〈出關〉的主角"老子"說：「我橫豎沒有牙齒，咬不動。」或者，《故事新編》中〈理水〉的"愚人"說：「真也比螺螄殼裏道場還難」暗喻極困難。這些語言具有歷史懷舊感的鄉土氣圍，也就形成了一種少見的諧趣，應該說這是魯迅完整清晰地表達了個人創作的風格，文字間偶爾也透露出英雄式的樂觀精神。

總而言之，研究魯迅小說不同於科學，科學是一種知識或理論能力。而魯迅把審美現象中的矛盾揭露出來，儘管他最終並未能有效地解決中國人的陋習、也無力改造積弊的社會。然而，魯迅一生不但精通日、德、俄等語言、熟識中國古典詩詞外，散文、翻譯、評論等創作之影響源遠流長。尤以小說為最，常能赤誠的吶喊，既有真情，又有形象。此外，魯迅小說中的美感，雖是感情經驗，卻具有理性基礎。他在中國小說歷史上的地位多半無人質疑，但也由於有時在文字表現的批判上過於犀利，強烈呈現反封建色彩，雖未走到個人主義的極端路線，還是在死後難逃被後世韃靼的命運。

蔡輝振在此書第六章第二節裡,明確地記錄下蘇雪林在《我論魯迅》中檢討了魯迅思想中的特異性。其中有段:「魯迅心理是病態的,性格大家公認是陰賊、刻薄、氣量偏狹、多疑善妒、復仇心堅韌強烈、領袖慾旺盛,思想陰暗空虛、憎恨哲學,可以說是個虛無哲學者,他的學力文才僅及叔本華、尼采、陀思妥耶夫斯基等人的一半。」後來又批評說魯迅是"流氓"、"土匪"等激憤之詞。

曾記得法國存在主義者沙特 Satre 的哲學觀點,他認為人生是絕對的自由,是可以完全的選擇。在選擇時,可以真誠的面對自己,也可欺騙自己。筆者以為,魯迅生前是把精神的自由當作創作的最高原則,在他眼底,雖然並不贊成尼采〈Nietzsche 1844-1900〉的充滿懷疑主義和虛無主義的翻譯哲學,但魯迅與尼采都有多災多難的人生經歷和孤獨的心靈,似存有心靈相通的一面;所以,魯迅對一生都被病痛和孤獨所折磨的天才尼采的理論是有選擇的接受的。至於魯迅的才氣是否如蘇雪林或其他批評者所說那般,則見人見智。

筆者以為,魯迅在付出自己畢生的精力後,他仍企圖透過文學將中國的苦痛與絕望反射出來,盼能重新建構一種新氣象;這就是他在小說裡所要表現的有關人性的掙扎與博鬥,怎不令人敬佩他的作法?他的小說,文如行雲流水,是中國現代語言的肯定,文字之中有一種對時代無限抗力的持續或嘲諷,或幽默或無奈心酸,也蘊含著某些喻象與力量。至於其它的翻譯文學及創作,也是為了絕大多數人的熱愛和一份孤獨的尊嚴而寫的。當然,這也並非全然無缺憾,魯迅有時憤恨的情緒,混雜了難以言說的苦味,字語間難免偏激,抑是更陷於孤獨和寂寞。然而,相信有智慧的讀者,當能體會魯迅敢於創造生存的希望,這份勇氣,畢竟是現代小說家們少有的現象。至於如果他的才氣不是如此,那歷史將被剪下這些片斷的頌揚和欽讚的。

三、結語:含蓄的批評

今年十一月初,收到蔡輝振寄來的《魯迅小說研究》時,讚美的呼聲迎接著他的這本學術著作,但同時也要指出其中的優缺:

其一、作者在研究方法上,引述分析、歸納,雖企圖統一他從前人學說中所看到的論述,卻未能完全如他所願。他只作到將魯迅小說的文獻整理分析的程度,象徵地試圖在各家批評之聲浪中,僅提出對未來研究方向的期許,並未能深入調和各家之說,或就魯迅小說的觀點,提出更創新的評論。

其二、在研究文本的態度上,蔡輝振的科學精神及務實態度是絕對無庸置疑的;我們可看出作者在求知過程時所下的苦功。他十分重視魯迅小說人物的歷史性,也逐步地探索魯迅創作的時代背景和性格形成的內在過程。他運用許許多多有關魯迅小說的寫作技巧,把故事的情節摘錄下來,在其思想的探討及藝術風格的塑造上,都表現得非常成功。

綜上而言,魯迅已經離開我們整整74年了,世界的潮流無止境的、又繼續向前逐流。如果要真正瞭解魯迅小說的價值性,就必須要去揭示他心理活動的奧祕。這既是剖析的根本目的,也是近幾十年來各學派對其正負面評價問題的癥結。筆者以為,除分析魯迅的潛意識、動機及人格等更深一層的內容外,其中,魯迅的美學思想遠比其意識生活更為重要。

從科學背景看,魯迅重視文學的力量是為企圖解決中國當時社會的病態現象、為改變民族的劣根性。這就反映出他是位有強度和有效率的心理系統。他的人格的形成並不是一個無衝突的徑直的過程，相反的，他因幼年家庭遭變故及外在環境的影響，確是一個充滿矛盾憤慨與悲涼的過程，也嘗盡世間冷暖。尤其是他的奉母成婚的悲劇婚姻，更讓他感到人生的孤寂與無奈。他曾說：「愛情是我所不知道的。」然而，在他的小說裡似乎也可以找到愛和建設性的能量；而且還成為創造用白話文寫小說的重要動力。魯迅十分推崇屈原著作《離騷》中的"浪漫的愛國精神"，也很喜歡幫助年輕人於求知。在文藝的本質上，他的文學正是中國國力衰微時期對於人性的尊嚴與藝術美的頌歌。他開闢了中國最早用西式新體寫小說的新領域，用文學去說明歷史、見證歷史。他的翻譯文學也通達流暢，堅持忠實原文，又力爭文字優雅風範。

　　依照這些觀點，筆者以為魯迅的美學思想就是他創造小說的主要表徵，對他的一生命運具有決定性的意義。魯迅的童年愛好閱讀較有趣味的野史、漫畫小說；也透過聽祖母說故事，開始著意把美、藝術與故事內容聯繫起來。這就不難看出，他的美學思想性格主導了日後創作的表現。而他在詩學上，也有種突發的藝術直覺，這是非有大氣魄、大力量的人所不能的。

　　再從小說的創作角度看，少有不具情感價值的東西。在德國美學家黑格爾〈Hegel,1770~1831〉的《美學》書中，即把藝術直覺稱為「充滿敏感的觀照。」他有句名言：「美是一種無目的快樂。」也可解釋說，心靈的愉悅才是最重要的。如果筆者對魯迅小說的上述理解合乎實際的話，那麼我認為閱讀魯迅小說，對絕大部份的人來說，仍是中國現代小說中對美學表現相當完整、最龐大也最確切的表述。它源生於魯迅感性與理性思維的完整的統一，在美學思想上，是一種最輕

靈的飛躍。最後,僅以一首詩致魯迅—這位掌握白話文學的優秀舵手:

〈兩后的夜晚〉

雪松寂寂
風裏我
聲音在輕喚著沉睡的星群
梧桐也悄然若思

路盡處,燈火迷茫
霧中
一個孤獨的身影
靜聽蟲鳴

雕像上的歌雀
狡點又溫熙地環伺著
突然,一陣樂音
隨夜幕飛來…拉長了小徑

——〈觀上海魯迅公園有感〉
寫於 2010.11.23 夜

——佛光大學文學院中國歷史學會《史學集刊》,第 43 集,2011 年 10 月,發表書評〈評蔡輝振的《魯迅小說研究》〉,頁 181-190。

國家圖書館出版品預行編目資料

```
宋詩明理接千載——古今抒情詩三百首（漢英對照）/
林明理 著、張智中 譯 －初版－
臺中市：天空數位圖書 2024.10
面：14.8*21 公分
ISBN：978-626-7576-00-7（平裝）
831                                    113015015
```

書　　　名：宋詩明理接千載——古今抒情詩三百首（漢英對照）
發 行 人：蔡輝振
出 版 者：天空數位圖書有限公司
作　　者：林明理
譯　　者：張智中
美工設計：設計組
版面編輯：採編組
出版日期：2024 年 10 月（初版）
銀行名稱：合作金庫銀行南台中分行
銀行帳戶：天空數位圖書有限公司
銀行帳號：006—1070717811498
郵政帳戶：天空數位圖書有限公司
劃撥帳號：22670142
定　　價：新台幣 490 元整
電子書發明專利第　I　306564　號
※如有缺頁、破損等請寄回更換

版權所有請勿仿製

服務項目：個人著作、學位論文、學報期刊等出版印刷及DVD製作
影片拍攝、網站建置與代管、系統資料庫設計、個人企業形象包裝與行銷
影音教學與技能檢定系統建置、多媒體設計、電子書製作及客製化等
TEL　　：(04)22623893　　　　MOB：0900602919
FAX　　：(04)22623863
E-mail ：familysky@familysky.com.tw
Https ://www.familysky.com.tw/
地　　址：台中市南區忠明南路 787 號 30 樓國王大樓
No.787-30, Zhongming S. Rd., South District, Taichung City 402, Taiwan (R.O.C.)